"It Can't Be, Hazzard. No Way Could It Be Her. Not After All These Years."

But ever the optimist, an image of Maggie Adams, a prickly and pouty enigma who had been just this side of perfect, drifted through his mind.

At least she'd been perfect to a smart-aleck seventeen-year-old. Back then, he'd been ruled by a healthy ego, raging hormones and a heart that had throbbed like a kettle drum every time he'd come within ogling distance of her thick chestnut hair, her brown-eyed glare and her long, luscious legs.

Lord, those legs. He used to fantasize about those legs. The last time he'd seen them in the flesh was that summer fifteen years ago—there on the very dock where his libido had just convinced his brain he'd seen them today.

He scoped out the bay, rechecked the wind and decided on an approach. No way was he flying off into the wild blue without checking this out....

Dear Reader,

Cowboys and cops...sexy men with a swagger...just the kind of guys to make your head turn. *That's* what we've got for you this month in Silhouette Desire.

The romance begins when Taggart Jones meets his match in Anne McAllister's wonderful MAN OF THE MONTH, *The Cowboy and the Kid.* This is the latest in her captivating CODE OF THE WEST miniseries. And the fun continues with Mitch Harper in *A Gift for Baby,* the next book in Raye Morgan's THE BABY SHOWER series.

Cindy Gerard has created a dynamic hero in the *very* masculine form of J. D. Hazzard in *The Bride Wore Blue,* book #1 in the NORTHERN LIGHTS BRIDES series. And if rugged rascals are your favorite, don't miss Jake Spencer in Dixie Browning's *The Baby Notion,* which is book #1 of DADDY KNOWS LAST, Silhouette's new cross-line continuity. (Next month, look for Helen R. Myers's *Baby in a Basket* as DADDY KNOWS LAST continues in Silhouette Romance!)

Gavin Cantrell is sure to weaken your knees in *Gavin's Child* by Caroline Cross, part of the delightful BACHELORS AND BABIES promotion. And Jackie Merritt—along with hero Duke Sheridan—kicks off her MADE IN MONTANA series with *Montana Fever.*

Heroes to fall in love with—and love scenes that will make your toes curl. That's what Silhouette Desire is all about. Until next month—enjoy!

All the best,

Lucia Macro

Senior Editor

Please address questions and book requests to:
Silhouette Reader Service
U.S.: 3010 Walden Ave., P.O. Box 1325, Buffalo, NY 14269
Canadian: P.O. Box 609, Fort Erie, Ont. L2A 5X3

CINDY GERARD
THE BRIDE WORE BLUE

SILHOUETTE *Desire*

Published by Silhouette Books

America's Publisher of Contemporary Romance

This book is dedicated to Debbie Sheets, Patti Knoll,
Glenna McReynolds and Anna Eberhardt. Every writer
should be so blessed to have such special friends to turn to
for strength, support and inspiration.
My special thank you to Greg Gunderson for answering a
multitude of questions about his beautiful 1956 Cessna.
And to Mike Deroma—thanks for the terrific ride!

 SILHOUETTE BOOKS

ISBN 0-373-76012-4

THE BRIDE WORE BLUE

Books by Cindy Gerard

Silhouette Desire

The Cowboy Takes a Lady #957
Lucas: The Loner #975
The Bride Wore Blue #1012

CINDY GERARD's

idea of heaven is a warm sun, a cool breeze, pan pizza and a good book. If she had to settle for one of the four, she'd opt for the book with the pizza running a close second. Inspired by the pleasure she's received from the books she's read and her long-time love affair with her husband, Tom, Cindy now creates her own sensual, evocative stories about compelling characters and complex relationships.

All that reading must have paid off because since winning the Waldenbooks Award for Bestselling Series Romance For a First-Time Author, Cindy has gone on to claim numerous awards, among them the prestigious Colorado Romance Writer's Award of Excellence and the coveted National Readers' Choice Award.

NORTHERN LIGHTS
BRIDES TRILOGY

Northern Minnesota is a land of sparkling glacial lakes and forests that stretch as far as the eye can see. Fortunately, civilization has not yet marred its remote beauty. In any given spot, on any given lake, images of free-spirited Indian warriors riding spotted ponies through the tree line come unbidden, as the past collides with the present.

Shadows of turn-of-the-century French fur traders and hardworking loggers weave like the wind through the pine. At night, in a secluded bay, when the moon dances on the water and the stars shimmer in an inky sky, the Aurora Borealis mystifies, intensifying the sense of wonder in this very special place.

Come with us to Legend Lake, where its people are as in tune with the North Country's uncompromising beauty as they are enmeshed in the past. And like many before them, become enamored by the mystery of the Northern Lights.

Experience the beauty, and live all three captivating romances in the NORTHERN LIGHTS BRIDES TRILOGY as they unfold.

One

The sky was baby blanket blue, the wind a crisp fifteen knots. It was a perfect day for flying, but any day he was in the air was perfect as far as J. D. Hazzard was concerned.

"Right, Hershey?" He grinned at his four-year-old chocolate lab, who loved flying, pizza and chasing squirrels, in that order.

Hershey, his tongue lolling comically from the side of his mouth, dutifully glanced J.D.'s way, then poked his nose back out the window.

"Right," J.D. confirmed, echoing his own sentiments. He lost his enthusiasm in the next breath, however, as the reason for this particular flight came back into play.

He set his mouth in a hard, tight line. Of all the jobs he had volunteered his services and those of his vintage four-seater Cessna for, this one he could do without. At least he could do without the reason for it—especially since he hadn't had any luck finding the low-life poachers he was looking for.

Give him fire spotting, blast patrols on the Iron Range or search and rescue any day. Hunting poachers was never easy. This particular gang was the worst of their kind. They were cagey and sly and totally without remorse. If he had his way, he'd see the whole miserable lot hung out to dry before they killed another black bear for profit.

"You gotta find 'em first," he reminded himself grimly. It didn't look like it was going to be today, though, he realized when the engine missed, then missed again.

Frowning, he decided he'd better call it quits and made a mental note to check the rocker arms after he landed. When he recognized the bay below him, though, he opted to circle the familiar inlet before packing it in.

"For old time's sake," he told himself, and let a wistful grin override his scowl. Old times and sweet times, he added as memories of a certain summer made him forget his foul mood.

It had been a long time since he'd wandered back to this end of Legend Lake. Longer still since he'd been a kid begging his dad for the keys to the boat so he could motor down the north shore, round the point and cruise into Blue Heron Bay.

Had it really been fifteen years? Diana Ross and Lionel Ritchie had been romancing the pop charts and the nation with "Endless Love." J.D. had been endlessly and hopelessly in love himself—with the longest legs and the prettiest brown eyes known to God, man or imagination.

"You didn't stand a chance in hell with her," he reminded himself with a self-deprecating sigh as he pictured Maggie Adams, a sixteen-year-old siren who wouldn't give him the time of day. Not back then. Not with his ego and his hormones outdistancing any attempt at *cool*.

"Lord, were you a jerk," he muttered with a full body shiver of disgust and a hindsight that had him shaking his head.

Another pronounced engine sputter knocked him back to the moment. He needed to head back to the base at Crane Cove Marina. One final, nostalgic look at the bay, however, had him doing a double take.

"What the hell . . ." he muttered when he spotted a figure on the dock.

Coaxing the aircraft's temperamental and now actively missing engine into a wide, banking turn, he buzzed the bay again. He cut speed, dropped swiftly to a couple hundred feet and confirmed what he thought he'd seen.

It was a woman. And from the looks of it, a pretty one, doing what pretty women do when faced with water, sun and time on their hands.

She was stretched out on the dock, soaking up some rays. Her sleek one-piece swimsuit was neon blue and second-skin snug. And her legs... Damn. Would you look at those legs. Even from here, they seemed to stretch on forever. The last time he'd seen legs like those . . .

The thought sputtered like his engine, then surged back to life with a growing, yet disbelieving excitement. The last time he'd seen legs like those, they'd been attached to Maggie Adams.

"It can't be, Hazzard," he told himself, even as he knuckled under to a sweet anticipation that had his pulse pumping like a piston. "You couldn't be that lucky. No way could it be her. Not after all these years."

But the hope hung tight, growing as big as the sky and twice as compelling. Ever the optimist, wishful thinking outdistanced the improbable as an indelible image of Maggie, a prickly and pouty enigma who to his eyes had been just this side of perfect, drifted through his mind like a strong, potent drug.

At least she'd been perfect to a smart-assed seventeen-year-old, he thought with a derisive grin. Back then, he'd been ruled by a healthy ego, raging hormones and a heart that had throbbed like a kettle drum every time he'd come within ogling distance of her thick chestnut hair, her brown-eyed glare and her long, luscious legs.

Lord, those legs. Though it had been a while, he used to dream about those legs. Fantasize about those legs. The last time he'd seen them in the flesh was that summer fifteen years ago—there on the very dock where his libido had just convinced his brain he'd seen them today.

Banking a sweet and escalating anticipation, he scoped out the bay, rechecked the wind and decided on an approach. No way in hell was he flying off into the wild blue without checking this out.

"Hang on, Hershey," he said, hearing far more excitement in his voice than a man who'd experienced and enjoyed a number of women had cause to. "We're about to pay the lady—whoever she is—a visit."

Distant, intrusive, like the low, monotonous buzz of a pesky mosquito, the sound drifted in on a lazy lake breeze, infiltrating a quiet she'd come to relish. She tried to tune it out. It wouldn't go away.

It was a plane, she finally realized with a scowl. While the location of the lake placed it well off any flight path, it wasn't unheard of to see the occasional private or hired float plane cruising the skies of the north country. Unusual was the fact that this one sounded so close.

With a deep, irritated breath, she dragged herself reluctantly out of her perfect peace and opened her eyes.

The sun, a glazing ball of baking warmth in an endless ocean of blue, had her groping blindly along the weathered planks of the dock for her dark glasses. Finding them, she slipped them on without sitting up, then searched the sky.

It didn't take long to spot the aircraft. It was a small, single-engine float plane. And not only was it close, it was *too* close, too low, and, it came to her with a sudden lurch of her heart when a series of sputters and coughs interrupted the engine's buzzing drone, in big trouble.

"Sweet Lord," she whispered, jackknifing to a sitting position. Her heart stalled, skipped, then slammed against her ribs before shifting into hard, heavy thuds when the engine missed, then missed again.

He was coming down.

Too fast, too fast, was all she could think as she watched the white wings and silver fuselage drop from the sky at a steep, dangerously reckless angle.

"Get on top of it," she willed the pilot as she scrambled to her feet. Shaking her eyes against the glare of the sun bouncing off water, she held her breath, afraid to watch, afraid not to. Her heart danced in her throat as the plane skipped once, again, then settled like a big white bird onto the glassy calm surface of the bay.

She let out a long breath of relief, then shook her head in admiration. She'd logged more than her share of jet time over the years, but beyond buckling in and praying for a safe takeoff and landing, she didn't know a thing about flying. She didn't have to to know that the pilot had accomplished a major miracle.

As the plane taxied farther into the bay and she could make out not only the numbers on the tail but the fact that baling wire, yards of silver tape and a heavy reliance on luck were about the only things holding the plane together, she traded her admiration for anger.

The fool. Anyone with both oars in the water wouldn't have been flying around in that beat-up relic to begin with. Up close and personal it was apparent that it had been a long time since the float plane had seen better days.

"Northlanders," she muttered, already pegging the pilot as a local. It only made sense. They were a different breed of cat, the whole reckless lot of them.

Though she'd kept to herself, and her association with the sturdy, adventurous people of the lake had been limited during the two months she'd been here, she'd learned that there wasn't a boat they wouldn't float, not a mountain they wouldn't climb, not a dare they wouldn't face down. She'd grown to love the people. She just wished she understood them and their reckless disregard for safety.

And why was the plane heading for *my* dock? she wondered crossly as it taxied slowly yet purposefully toward her. There were six other cabins spaced around the point. All of them were closer than hers. A few were occupied for the weekend. Some had phones—which she, by design, did not. She was here to get away from it all, not invite it in with electronics, fiber optics or conversation.

"Or fools in flight gear," she muttered with a deepening scowl.

Why my dock?

The question played back again, niggling like a paper cut. Only this time, the mystery triggered unease instead of irritation. She'd been so concerned about the pilot making it down safely, she'd forgotten to be worried about herself. She'd let her guard down. It was a disturbing mental lapse she couldn't afford—not if she wanted to ensure her solitude. And her safety, she added with a reluctant concession to an ugly piece of reality she hadn't ever come to terms with.

With concentrated effort, she made herself stay put and reason out the situation. Rolfe would never think of looking for her here. He didn't know about the cabin. No one did. No one could possibly know she was here. She'd covered her tracks too well. If someone found her it would be because she'd decided it was time to be found—and that was the million-dollar dilemma. She wasn't sure if that time would ever come.

She studied the plane as it floated closer. It's just some hot-shot Northlander who was out on a joy ride and ran into trouble, she told herself rationally. Steeped in that conviction, she finally convinced herself she'd momentarily overreacted. What she was dealing with here was some local yokel with a death wish and less than optimum gray matter. Though her anxiety abated, her scowl deepened as she crossed her arms beneath her breasts and waited while the wake generated from the landing washed the plane closer.

By the time the plane's left float hit soundly against the wooden dock piling and the motor hiccuped to a stop, she'd decided to give the pilot a piece of her mind before she sent him on his way. Only her mind wasn't up to sparing any parts when she got a look at the man who shouldered open the complaining cabin door.

He was a local all right. A born and bred by-product of hearty Finn and Swede ancestry who had settled this wild and beautiful country almost a hundred years ago. His Scandinavian lineage was so apparent that even before he looked up at her, slowly slipping off his mirrored aviator sunglasses, she'd known the eyes behind them would be blue.

Blue didn't quite cover it, though, she was forced to admit, when she instinctively met his gaze. Blue was an understatement. A paltry description when faced with such a true, stunning hue. The sky was somehow captured in his eyes. The sky and the water, and the myriad shades that each could reflect on the most brilliant summer day.

She wasn't prepared for the size of him, either, or for his bearing as he propped his sunglasses on top of a head of hair the color of toasted gold, clasped a strong, tanned hand around a leather grip attached above the cockpit doorway and hauled himself easily out of the cramped space.

He'd barely cleared the small opening and stepped onto a float when a huge brown dog scrambled out behind him. The wild ball of fur hit the float, then bounded onto the dock, nearly knocking her over in a desperate spring for the woods.

"Hershey!" he yelled, his deep voice scolding. When the dog just kept running, he gave her an apologetic shrug and nodded toward the spot in the tree line where the lab had disappeared into the dense forest. "Sorry. He usually has better manners. Guess it was past time for a tree break."

She assumed a defensive stance, determined not to let the dog's antics—or the man's bearing—sway her. "If he was as afraid as I was of you making it down in one piece, I'm surprised he didn't bail out sooner."

"What? Oh, that?" His brows drew together before he jerked his head toward the engine. "That's nothing a little tune-up can't fix."

He smiled at her then. Openly. Beautifully. And he just kept on smiling while she stood there armed only with a reluctant scowl that curiously wanted to ease into an answering grin.

It didn't make any sense. Besides giving her a good scare, she didn't find his attitude even marginally acceptable. His "well, well, what have we here" arrogance—even though good-natured—seemed to size her up in one practiced and perfected glance.

He was a cocky son of a gun, she concluded, her frown locking a little tighter as he turned back toward the cockpit. While he fiddled around, searching for something under the seat, she took the opportunity to catalog her immediate impressions.

His total lack of pretense completely put to rest any lingering concern that Rolfe might have sent him. Despite his size and unscheduled appearance, there was something about him that stated unequivocally that what you saw is what you got. No hidden agenda. No ulterior motives. Besides, subtlety wasn't Rolfe's style. If he'd found out she was here, he'd have come after her himself.

This man wasn't anybody's flunky. His black T-shirt and tight, worn jeans did little to conceal the measure of the man he was. Viking blond and Paul Bunyan brawn, he was six-two if he was an inch. The quintessential Norse god, comfortable with his power, confident of his effect on women.

His jaw was firm and angular, his mouth full and wide, and as he ducked under a wing strut, swung around to face her fully and jumped onto the dock, a fat roll of silver tape clutched loosely in his big, tanned hand, that very mouth was still set in that exasperatingly expectant grin.

She shivered involuntarily, feeling both the warmth of fire and the cool of melting ice as he searched her face, then made a lazy, assessing sweep of her body from her head to her bare toes. When he met her eyes again, the corners of his were crinkled with a smug, warm pleasure and that infectious expectancy that should have put her on guard but somehow managed to intrigue her.

She slipped off her dark glasses to get a better read on the situation. If possible, his grin expanded the moment she did.

Balancing his weight on one long, muscular leg, he crossed his arms over his chest and let go of a satisfied sigh.

"Well, hell," he said, drawing the words out in a voice that was honey thick, bourbon mellow and as warm as the afternoon sun. "It *is* you. Son of a gun," he murmured, as if he couldn't believe his good fortune. "How are ya, Stretch? It's been a while."

Stretch? With a sideways tilt of her head, she stared deeper as memories, muddied by time, shifted and skidded and finally blended into something she could latch on to.

She was used to being recognized, but not by that name. Only one person she knew had ever called her Stretch and she hadn't actually considered him a *person* back then. The only resemblance that pencil-thin boy bore to the man grinning as if he'd won the lottery was his height and his eyes. And the size of his feet. Long and sturdy, his tan feet, void of socks, filled what she'd guess were size-thirteen

high-tops that were more worn than his jeans. Judging
from the look of them, they were held together by a wish
and a prayer and several inches of the same silver tape that
appeared to be holding his plane together.

It couldn't be, she told herself, giving him another long,
considering look. Fifteen years ago she'd considered him
more of a subspecies, a card-carrying cretin and a royal
pain in the tush. He'd teased and tormented and proposi-
tioned her until she'd wanted to tie an anchor around his
scrawny neck and toss him into the bay.

She frowned, dug deeper and tried again to find a scrap
of something familiar. The raging hormone who had
shadowed her steps like a lust-struck puppy had been all
sharp, skinny angles, smart irreverent mouth and school-
boy swagger. Reminding her back then of the great Blue
Heron who had given the bay its name, she'd tagged him
"Blue" to get back at him for the label he'd pinned on her
and her own long-legged form.

"Blue?" An odd mixture of disbelief and reluctant
pleasure cluttered her thoughts as she searched his smiling
face again. "Blue Hazzard? Is it really you?"

Her slow, astonished realization seemed to tickle him.
"As if the world could handle another."

"My Lord." She couldn't stop the smile this time.
Shaking her head, she extended her hand. "After all these
years. I don't believe it."

His grin just got wider. And more focused. And if possible, more attractive.

"Fifteen years," he murmured, shaking his head before
adding with obvious approval, "You haven't changed,
Stretch." He gave her another one of those maddeningly
male once-overs as he folded her hand in his firm, possessive grip. "Not by so much as an eyelash."

She was used to being sized up, cataloged and price-
tagged. She was used to the unforgiving eye of the camera.
It came with the territory. It was part of the cost of suc-

cess. But Blue's bold, steady appraisal made her uncomfortably aware of all the bare skin exposed by her skimpy suit. To combat the feeling, she drew her hand way from his and slipped her sunglasses back in place.

"Well, *you* have," she managed with no staged amazement as she tried to deal with the heat his grip had generated and the alarming and totally uncalled for thunder of her heart.

She tucked her hands around her waist, distancing herself and downplaying her reaction to him. His gaze remained fixed on her face, confident, penetrating.

"*Some* things haven't changed, though." She nodded toward the plane, taking a much-needed break from the eye contact. He'd always told her he was going to fly some day. Of course, he'd always told he was going to do a lot of things—like break down her resistance and get her into the back seat of his daddy's car. "It would appear you're still sticking your neck out and courting disaster."

He followed her gaze to the Cessna. His face lit up with pride and affection. "She's a beauty, isn't she?"

"A beauty?" She couldn't stop a skeptical chuckle. "You always were optimistic to a fault. Not to burst your bubble, but there are some children only a father could love. In case you really hadn't noticed, that plane is a wreck."

That was stating the obvious. The plane needed more than a coat of paint to make it respectable again. And from the sound of the engine when he'd set it down, an oilcan and a screwdriver wouldn't amount to much more than a bandage surgery.

He managed a playfully affronted scowl. "You can't be serious? Surely you can see past the surface to the buried treasure beneath." He shot another adoring look toward the Cessna. "She's vintage."

"And dangerous. Next you'll tell me it runs better than it sounds."

"Don't let her sputtering fool you. She's just a little cranky today." Those Nordic blue eyes took another long, leisurely side trip up and down the length of her bare legs. *Like you,* his look implied. "Nothing a little special attention can't fix."

Also implied was the suggestion that he could take care of Maggie's crankiness, too—with a little special attention.

"Believe me," he added, all charm and choirboy innocence when she bristled, "she's in much better shape than she looks. *You,* on the other hand..." He stopped, devouring her with his eyes again with a thoroughness that made her feel like she'd just been swallowed whole. "You look about as good as good can get."

And he looked incredible, she admitted reluctantly, still astonished as she pitted memory against the improbable reality of the present. Who'd have ever thought that the gangly combination of knees, elbows and Adam's apple that was Blue Hazzard would have turned into this model-perfect specimen.

With or without the smile, despite the arrogance, he was ruggedly handsome, strikingly blond. The dark tint of his skin—a rich, sun-baked bronze, unmistakably natural and a welcome change from the salon-bed tans she was used to seeing—told of his love of the outdoors. The length of his hair—unacceptable by boardroom standards yet styled beautifully by wind and weather into an artful and totally disarming disarray—told of his uncommon and unconscious disregard for the picture he made standing there.

In a world—in *her* world, anyway—of fabricated beauty and augmented perfection, he was a rarity. The real thing, not the eight-by-ten glossy image produced and perfected by the masters of glitz for the high-ticket, high-profile business she was used to. And because he was so real, it was impossible not to appreciate the obvious: this man was all length, all strength, and all male.

They'd love him in New York. They'd eat him alive. Or at least they'd try. Just like they'd tried with her, she thought grimly. Sometimes she wondered if they hadn't succeeded.

"What?" he asked, reacting to her distant, thoughtful look.

Realizing he'd caught her staring, she shot him a tight smile, then shrugged. "I don't know. I was just remembering, I guess. I still can't believe it's you. You...you were such a..."

"Jerk?" he supplied with a helpful look, then followed up with a chuckle. The sound was as warm as the sun and as engaging as his smile, which was automatic and devastating. "Some say I still am."

"And are they right?"

She wasn't sure why she was letting him lead her into this wordplay. It was both unwarranted and untimely. She didn't want to renew old acquaintances. She didn't want to open the door and invite him in to even this little piece of her life. She didn't even like him. At least she didn't like the Blue Hazzard she remembered.

"Are they right?" He echoed her question as he took a slow, purposeful step toward her. "I guess you're going to have to tell me." Cupping her shoulder in his huge, warm hands, he drew her unerringly toward him. "Because I'm about to put it to the test.

"I've waited fifteen years for this, Stretch." His face relayed a devastating combination of reflection, seduction and unshakable intent. "Fifteen years is a long time to make good on a promise."

Sensing what he was about to do, she felt helpless to back away from him—for reasons too numerous to catalog and impossible to understand. "Promise?" she whispered, riveted by the heat in his eyes and the sensual blend of strength and gentleness of his hold.

"I promised myself that if I ever saw you again, I'd do what I ached to do back then but didn't have the guts to pull off."

Before she could decide if she should be frightened, angry or excited, or all three, he lowered his mouth to hers.

Two

He didn't give her the time to search for the strength of mind and body to stop this. He didn't give her the option. As he dipped his head and his mouth sought hers, the thought did register that she shouldn't be letting it happen. The warning bells rang and her fight-or-flight instincts surged to the surface only to sink in the depths and beyond the moment Blue Hazzard's mouth touched hers.

Reverence. Maggie felt reverence and tenderness and the pleasure of a promise held too long in trust.

If she gave a struggle, it was token. If she voiced a protest, it was unconvincing, as any notion of denying him lost power and proportion under his gently persuasive touch.

Blue Hazzard was kissing her. And she was letting him. Letting him coax her surrender with the heat of his lips against hers, with the caress of his hands on her shoulders. Hands that were huge and strong yet achingly gentle as they glided surely down her back then drew her close against his body. A body that was as solid as the rock gouging out the shoreline, as warm as the sun enfolding them both.

Ebb and flow, soft and slow, the water lapped against the dock beneath them as he savored her there in the sunlight, there in the wilderness where she'd come to escape pressure and indecision and the disabling suffocation of involvement, which, for her, equated to control.

Yet here, wrapped in this man's arms, she felt free, adrift in poignant memories of simpler times. Embraced by the promise that with him it might be different. And she rediscovered the fever of arousal at its finest. Steady and mellow. Sheltered and safe, yet wildly sensual and shockingly erotic.

And over.

In a daze, she opened her eyes.

Lazy with contentment, heavy with desire, he searched her face before bringing his hand to her sunglasses and slipping them back to the top of her head.

"Ah, Stretch," he whispered, brushing his thumb in a slow, tender caress along the rise of her flushed cheek. "I was a fool to have waited so long."

Then he took her mouth again. With a hunger that spoke of his desire. With an aggression that relayed his strength—and showed her lack of it.

Panic belatedly kicked in, hitting an all-time high on her warning meter. Her heart slammed against her chest as her instincts, wrenched to life by a swift and graphic memory of the pain and the power of another man's touch, threw her into action.

The hands she'd brought to his shoulders in a caress knotted into white-knuckled fists. The pleasure she'd felt only moments ago in his arms transformed to a staggering, blinding need to escape. She pushed wildly against him, shifting and twisting, fighting for her breath and her freedom.

"Hey . . . hey . . . easy." He let her go so abruptly that she stumbled back and would have landed on her rump if he hadn't reached out, caught her arm and steadied her.

"Easy, okay?" His voice, like his expression, was puzzled but soothing. Concern darkened his eyes even as he backed a step away, his hands open and held wide from his body, clearly showing her he was giving her room.

Wild-eyed, she stared at him, sucking air, digging deep for composure.

"You all right?" he asked, wary and pensive.

She pinched her eyes shut and gave a sharp nod. Forcing calm, she grounded herself with deep breaths, willing the panic to subside, feeling her heartbeat reluctantly even out.

When she thought she could handle it, she met his eyes. He was watching her with a measuring, uncertain silence that invited her to explain what had just happened.

It was an invitation she couldn't accept. Not now. Not from him. Maybe not from any man ever again.

Drawing on the strength that had gotten her to this point, she overpowered the last of her panic with anger. "They're right," she announced tightly.

He tilted his head, cocked a questioning brow.

"You're still a jerk, Hazzard. You never did understand 'no' unless I hit you over the head with it."

J.D. scowled. He understood no, all right. And no was not the answer she'd given him when he'd kissed her. Not the first time, at any rate. The first time, she'd said yes over and over again as their mouths met and mated and she'd invited him to take what he hadn't dared to dream she would offer. She'd answered with a yes as true as time and as sure as tomorrow.

"My mistake," he conceded anyway, giving her the room she seemed to need, catering to the panic he'd seen flashing in her eyes.

And it had been panic. Though diminished, or at least glossed over with irritation, it was still there, puzzling and heartbreaking and deflating the hell out of his ego.

He never lost sight of the fact that he was a big man. Because of it, he'd never given a woman reason to be afraid of him due to his size and strength. Instinctively, he knew that wasn't what was making her so skittish now. It was something else, something that had nothing to do with him.

"I always did make my share of mistakes around you." He forced a smile when what he wanted to do was pin down the real cause of her fear.

Hershey trotted out of the woods and onto the dock before he had the chance to ask her about it. J.D. watched in silence as Maggie took the opportunity to close off any possibility of a twenty-questions session. She went down on one knee and gave the lab the attention his slowly wagging tail and soulful brown eyes begged for.

Rubbing his jaw thoughtfully, J.D. simply observed as Maggie lavished soft words and generous affection on the adoring dog. The picture she made was one of complete control. And yet her hands were shaking. He worked his lower lip between a finger and thumb and made a decision to back off. For the time being, anyway. The lady clearly needed some time to pull herself together.

He didn't know what it was that had put the fear in her eyes but he was solid in the belief that it wasn't him. In the moment when their mouths and bodies had come together, fear had been the last thing on her mind. She'd reacted to him. Sure and swift and with a stunning combination of desire and need—a need so strong he'd felt an outrageous need of his own to protect her.

Protect, possess. Provide for.

Whoa. Back up the boat, Hazzard. Hormones, memories and long-ago summertime lust did not equate to the "P" words, which in turn equated to commitment—not after a fifteen-year absence. Hell, they'd both been kids then.

He let his gaze drift along her sun-bright hair and tanned skin and drew a deep, controlling breath. They definitely weren't kids anymore. While physically the changes in her appearance had been subtle—a lush and benevolent maturing of a youthful face and body—in other ways he could see much more pronounced differences. As he watched in intrigued silence as she buried her face in the lab's silky coat, he was suddenly very sorry he hadn't been around when those events had been molding her into the woman she was today. The Maggie he'd known had been tough and tart. She'd had a mouth made for kissing and put-downs and a mind set on independence.

In this life or the next, he'd never figured she would have turned into a woman who would let a little good-natured flirting upset her. If pressed, she might try to deny it with indifference, but he knew otherwise. She *had* been upset.

Okay. So he'd gone a little further than flirting. But she'd gone a lot further than being upset. She'd been scared to death. Yet, it had only been a kiss.

Wrong, Hazzard, he conceded. If it had only been a kiss, his heart wouldn't have skipped like the Cessna's engine on a nosedive. It wouldn't be going all mushy right now as he watched her try to get hold of herself.

Aw, Stretch. What the hell happened to you?

And what the hell had happened to him to make it so important that he find out?

Had to be the legs, Hazzard, he told himself on a lengthy, self-deprecating sigh. He'd always been a sucker for her legs. And her smile. And her tough-guy temperament that had had him stepping and fetching and panting like a marathon runner at the finish line.

Only he'd never crossed that line with her. Not back then. He'd never even come close.

He made an immediate and reckless decision then. Now that she was back on the scene—whatever the reason—there were a lot of lines he planned on crossing. Starting with why and how she had ended up back at the lake in the first place...and ending with what had put that hunted, haunted look in her eyes.

Before he could form his first question, though, her head came up. Her gaze skittered, as it had since he'd first stepped out of the plane, past his to the bay behind him.

"It might have been a good idea to tie up to the dock," she announced with an offhanded innocence that immediately set his senses on alert.

He frowned, glanced back over his shoulder, did a double take and swore roundly.

When he turned his glare back on her, she had the nerve to let a little grin tip up one corner of that delicious mouth.

While he'd stood there mooning over Maggie Adams like a love-struck teenager, the Cessna had very quietly floated a couple hundred yards out into the bay.

Without taking his eyes from hers, he stripped his T-shirt over his head and tossed it along with his sunglasses and the roll of duct tape onto the dock. "You watched it go, didn't you?"

She gave a noncommittal shrug that suggested she had taken perverse pleasure in doing just that.

"You could have said something," he muttered, hopping first on one foot, then the other as he shucked his shoes.

"I believe I just did."

Her smug little smile made him want to put her in her place. While he couldn't say he much cared for the pleasure she was deriving out of this—and all at his expense—he was glad the fear in her eyes had been replaced by a sassy spark of amusement. *This* was the Maggie he remembered.

"You'll pay for this, Stretch," he promised amiably, then extracted his first payment when he stripped off his jeans and stood before her in nothing but black silk boxers.

Her face turned the color of a red channel marker.

"You'll pay dearly," he assured her, flashing a warning grin. With a command to Hershey to stay, he dove into the bay.

Maggie stood and stewed and blasted herself for doing it. Yet she couldn't look away. With her arms crossed tightly under her breasts, she watched Blue swim out to the plane.

"He's managed to take care of himself the last fifteen years when you weren't around," she sputtered under her breath. "He doesn't need you fussing like a mother hen now."

With that thought, she forced herself to turn her back on him and the lake, and told herself she didn't care if he drowned on his merry way. He was going to end up killing himself eventually anyway if he piloted that plane many more times.

"Plane," she muttered darkly. "Flying leaky boat is more like it. Disaster with a prop. He and that contraption deserve each other."

Hershey's agitated woofs coming from where he stood vigil on the end of the dock had Maggie spinning on her heel, though, as visions of a Hazzardless bay and a few telltale bubbles outdistanced her resolve to ignore him.

Blue water and—thankfully—Blue Hazzard filled her field of vision, however, as he reached the plane and hefted his gorgeous self out of the water. Settling his hip onto the float, he whipped his head back, sending water flying in a sparkling crystal arc from that glorious mass of golden hair.

She felt a relief that was too swift and too sweet. And a flutter of arousal that hit like a thief in the night. He was a beautiful man, gilded in the sunlight from the top of his sun-streaked hair to the tawny glow of his tanned skin. He was male from the breadth of his shoulders to the symmetrical sculpting of his chest to his narrow hips and the fluid lines of his long, muscular legs. And just looking at him excited her.

Her swift, strong reaction stunned her. After Rolfe, she'd never intended to let a man affect her that way again. After Rolfe, she'd never thought it would be possible. Blue Hazzard had just proven her wrong. He'd not only managed to arouse a physical response, he'd managed to make her concerned about him.

Just her luck, he picked the exact moment her shoulders had straightened with both relief and awareness to catch her eye. He gave her a macho grin and a thumbs-up signal, then maneuvered smoothly to stand in all his wet, near-naked glory on the battered silver float.

"Jerk," she mumbled, irritated that she'd not only given in to her response to him but that she'd let him see it and recognize it for what it was.

The big question was why. Why did she react to him physically and why did she care about what happened to him? She didn't want to think about the physical part. The concern, however, she could reason out rationally. She'd watched the plane float away. She should have said something. Some perverse desire to tilt his world a little off kilter—just like he'd tilted hers—had prompted her to keep silent. Consequently, if something had happened to him— cramps were not out of the realm of possibility—it would have been her fault.

"Wrong," she stated firmly as she turned her back on him again and marched up the rock and grass path to the cabin. "Don't fall into that trap again. That's the kind of twisted rationale you came here to get away from. It would not have been your fault. It would have been his fault for not tying the plane to the dock in the first place."

Slipping into the cabin through the back screen door, she walked directly to the bedroom. She peeled off her suit, snagged panties and a bra, then stepped into khaki walking shorts and a red tank top. Then she proceeded to ignore the fact that there was a dog on her dock, a plane in her bay and a near-naked man responsible on both counts.

It wasn't that she was deluding herself into thinking she'd gotten rid of him. Not yet. It was just that when she confronted him again, it was going to be with the benefit of at least one of them fully clothed.

Maybe then she wouldn't experience this undercurrent of awareness muddling up her system. And maybe then her face wouldn't heat up at just the thought of Blue Hazzard stripping to his skivvies and displaying his long, muscular legs, slim hips and broad, tanned chest for her benefit.

"*Conceited* jerk," she grumbled, adding to his list of transgressions as she stalked to the picture window and pretended she wasn't interested in what he was up to.

The swim to the plane had been a no-sweat proposition. J.D. kept in shape, as much for himself as out of necessity. Coaxing the cantankerous engine to a disgruntled, wheezing start, however, was another story.

He wheedled, he pleaded. He prayed and promised. He even whimpered a little, and finally she gave in and humored him. Babying her along, whispering sweet nothings, hoping that if she decided to cut out on him before he made it back to the dock that the momentum would take her the rest of the way, he taxied slowly back toward an anxious Hershey—and an absent Maggie.

"Run, little rabbit," he whispered toward the cabin, where he figured she'd burrowed in to wait him out. "I've got all the time in the world."

Luck was with him. The engine didn't die until he bumped into the pilings. Jumping quickly onto the worn pine planks, he made the front of the float fast, then, skirting a tail-thumping Hershey, strode to the back of the plane and tied it securely, as well.

That done, and with a covert glance toward the cabin, he grabbed his jeans and tugged them on. She thought he couldn't see her up there, but he could. Through the birch and pine that crowded twenty yards of sloping shoreline, he caught a glimpse of her silhouette as she paced by the picture window craning her neck to get a better look.

Good, he thought with a satisfied grin. She didn't want to be, but she was interested. He planned on letting her get an eyeful while her curiosity built.

He grabbed the roll of duct tape he'd tossed on the dock before his unscheduled dip in the sixty-eight degree water and tore off a strip. Positioning it securely over a crack in a riveted seam on the wingtip, he delivered on the first of his promises to the Cessna.

"See, baby? I promised I'd take care of you," he murmured as he smoothed the tape into place then snuck another glance toward the cabin.

"Let's let her stew, huh, Hersh?" he suggested softly as the lab nosed his head under his hand, begging for attention.

Squatting down on his haunches, he gave Hershey the ear-scratching he was angling for. "Never did meet a woman who wasn't just busting with curiosity and let it get the best of her before all was said and done."

Whistling softly between his teeth, he rose to his feet and stepped out onto a float. After a little shifting and tugging, he managed to dislodge the tool kit from under the pilot seat. He grinned when he felt the warm burn of her gaze couple with the eighty-degree sun on his bare back as he peeled back the strip of duct tape securing the engine cowling. Folding it back, he settled in to do a little minor repair work and a *lot* of creative tinkering while he waited her out.

"Conceited, *stalling* jerk," Maggie muttered under her breath as she checked the sun's descent toward the west where it would soon disappear in the trees behind her cabin.

She'd done her twenty-minute workout—old habits were hard to break. She'd showered. She'd made a pitcher of lemonade, then felt too guilty to have a cool glass while he sweltered down there in the hot sun. Finally, she drank a glass for spite just to prove to herself she didn't care what happened to him.

She sat by the window with a book but couldn't remember a thing she'd read because she'd spent most of her time alternately watching Blue and Hershey. The lab's antics made her smile as he skittered in and out of the woods, sometimes chasing a teasing chipmunk, sometimes wading into the water from the nearby beach to coax a lounging mallard into giving him a run for his money, sometimes lolling in the shade, his only movements the lazy slap of his tail when a fly pestered.

Blue's antics, however, made her frown as all the while she watched him, he puttered with his precious plane, never sparing a glance toward the cabin. She wasn't sure how that made her feel. She only knew his being here unsettled her.

He'd been down there for over three hours, messing with his tools, taping things together and spreading important-looking engine parts on her dock. It didn't look like he was close to packing up and winging his way out of her life any time soon. In fact, she noted, her scowl deepening as she gave up on the book and tossed it on an end table, he'd just laid another piece of greasy metal on the dock.

She sliced another impatient glance at the clock. It was almost six. While the July sun didn't completely disappear until nine or after this time of the year, she was getting a little nervous about whether he'd have the Cessna in working order before sunset. If he didn't, then what would she do with him? While it seemed to be his personal style, she doubted very much that he could fly that plane by night.

She pinched her mouth tight and bit on the inside of her cheek. Only when she realized what her frustration had driven her to—skulking around in the cabin to avoid him—

did she make a decision. She wasn't going to hide out any longer. Not here. Not because of him. Not in her own home.

Home. The word stalled, then settled comfortably when she realized she'd applied it to this little cabin in the north woods more than once since she'd been here. New York had been home for the past fourteen years. Yet after a short two-month span of time, this primitive cabin and the vast isolation of the Northland felt more like home than her upscale Soho co-op ever had.

"At least it *had* been isolated," she grumbled as her attention focused again on the man standing with his legs spread wide and his hands full of some mechanical mystery that was dripping oil and making him frown.

Wearing a frown of her own, she refilled her glass, then grudgingly filled another one. With a sigh that could have been resignation, determination, disgust or all three, she headed out the door.

J.D. was hot. He was also bored. He'd fixed the engine problem a couple of hours ago and he'd about run out of engine parts to tinker with when he finally heard the soft sound of approaching footsteps falling on the wooden dock.

"Thank you," he whispered skyward, then turned toward the sound, knowing he looked like a sap as his smile spread warm and welcoming. He couldn't help it. Didn't care. She looked so damn good walking toward him. She'd pulled her dark, shoulder-length hair from her face with a solid-gold hair band. Her cheeks and nose were rosy above her soft summer tan and today's kiss of the sun. But best of all, she was carrying two glasses full of ice-cold lemonade. That had to be a good sign.

"Hey," he said, wiping his hands on a rag and gladly taking the one she extended, in silence, to him. "This is just what the doctor ordered."

He hadn't realized just how hot he was. Or how dry. He felt the sweat trickle down his temple to blend with more on his neck as he tipped his head back and downed the entire contents of the glass in three huge, gulping swallows.

With a blissful sigh, he licked the last drop of liquid off the lip of the glass then dragged it across his bare chest to smooth the remains of the cooling moisture there. "Man. Did that hit the spot."

She looked from the empty glass to him and blinked.

He laughed. "Big man. Big thirst," he explained. "Bad manners," he said apologetically. "I'm sorry. I shouldn't have made such a pig of myself."

"I guess I shouldn't have left you out in the sun so long without something to drink. I'm the one who's sorry."

He considered her then. Her genuine regret. Her too-acute bearing of blame. And he wondered when this had become such a serious matter.

"You can make it up to me with another glass. Just like the other one," he added, giving her a huge grin.

Without a word, she retrieved his glass—greasy finger-prints and all—and headed back up the slope to the cabin.

By the time she returned with the refill, he'd managed to wipe the worst of the grime from his hands, tug on his T-shirt and drag a couple of dock chairs onto the grass and out of the sun.

She didn't want to get friendly. That was clear. But J.D. figured that shared memories and that combustible kiss they'd experienced earlier had taken them a little past what she wanted to a few unalterable facts. She may not *want* to get friendly, but she didn't have a prayer of forestalling it. He was going to make damn sure of that.

He stood by the chairs, waiting for her to sit. She hesitated, gave him a wary glance, then eased down into the old metal spring chair. Using her lemonade and Hershey as buffers between them, she ignored him as he sat, too, taking in the sight of her and wondering, still, at the reason she was here.

"Been a long time since I sat under this tree," he remarked with a wistful, melancholy look around him. "It was a nice surprise finding you here today. Real nice," he added with a soft, inviting smile.

"So what brings you back, Stretch?" he asked finally, when her extended silence told him nothing more than that she was reluctant to share even a little bit of herself with him.

Her quiet gaze skimmed the still waters of the bay, from the rocky shoreline directly ahead of them to the grassy shadows tucked like waving wheat in the breakwater protected by the dock and finally to the little beach nestled twenty yards to the west.

"I think the real question is what kept me away so long."

His gaze followed hers to the beauty, to the peace and the tranquillity that was the lake and the wonder that was this natural northern paradise, and he understood. "Got in your blood, didn't it?"

"Yeah," she said, her eyes drifting shut as the lake breeze played with her hair, lifting it gently from her brow and feathering it against her cheek. "It did."

They shared the silence then. The silence that was punctuated with the playful lap of water to shore, the distant call of the gulls and the hypnotic, muted chatter of a dozen pairs of summering mallards and their broods fishing and sunning themselves on the rocks near the beach.

He sat back in the old chair, letting his weight bow the springs. Rocking like an ancient to the lulling sounds of summer, he tried to figure out his good fortune and a safe way to get her to open up.

"So," he began, feeling his way carefully. "I figured a Caribbean beach or the French Riviera would have been more your speed for an exotic getaway."

There. It was out in the open. At the very least it was implied that he'd followed her career, or that he was aware of it. Who wasn't? Anyone who didn't live under a rock had to be aware of Maggie. He'd discovered Maggie, the superstar, super-sought-after supermodel by accident about seven years ago. He'd been sitting in a dentist's office, thumbing through some glitzy women's magazine out of sheer boredom when a lingerie ad had caught his eye. Caught his eye? Singed his eyeballs was more like it. The model was a knockout. A bona fide, jerk-your-heart-around, make-your-jeans-tight knockout.

His hands had stilled, then he'd folded the page out flat and stared, and devoured and forgotten all about his impending root canal as he fought to resurrect a memory that wouldn't quite come into focus.

He was under the drill, drifting on laughing gas and dreaming of summer love when it hit him and damn near knocked him out of the dental chair.

The Maggie in the magazine wasn't just the single-name phenomenon that little girls wanted to grow up to be like and big girls strived to copy. She was *his* Maggie. His Maggie Adams, who still had the ability to heat his blood to flash point with a single look from her spicy brown eyes. It was *his* Maggie who had been staring her stubborn, sultry, untouchable stare from the page of that magazine, wearing nothing but a white silk teddy and thigh-high lace stockings.

He looked over at her now. Her aristocratic yet sensual features were bare of makeup and pretense, her dark eyes were striking without benefit of shadows and shadings and carefully positioned lights and he thought she was still the most beautiful woman he'd ever seen.

"You've had a helluva ride, haven't you, Stretch?"

Still, she remained silent. And he wondered at the cause of it. Since that first time he'd discovered her in that ad, he'd seen her face and body on everything from magazine covers to billboards, to TV advertising, to a segment of "Lifestyles of the Rich and Famous," to promotions for her signature perfume. In the world of glamour and glitz, stars didn't rise any higher.

Yet, still she sat. Silent. Somber. Hanging on to her thoughts and her emotions like the glass she clenched tightly in her hands.

"How's the plane?" she asked finally, never meeting his eyes. "Are you going to be able to put it back together?"

And fly out of my life and leave me alone? was the trailing, unvoiced ending to that question that he guessed she was too polite to put into words.

So she didn't want to get chummy. So she didn't want him hanging around long enough to get reacquainted. Tough.

Most men would have taken the hint and left the lady alone. He wasn't most men. But then, Maggie Adams wasn't just any woman. She was *the* woman of his adolescent dreams. The embodiment of his perfect woman. And even though he hadn't realized it until he'd had the good luck to find her again today, she was the woman by whom he'd measured all others since and found them lacking.

Was he going to fly out of her life and leave her alone? Hell no. But since it seemed so important to her, he'd oblige her by making her think he was trying. The truth of the matter was, he wasn't going anywhere. Not yet. Not any time soon. He was determined to get her to open up to him.

Whether she liked it or not, he figured he'd stick around until then—or at least until he satisfied himself that she couldn't possibly be all he remembered and everything he'd ever wanted a woman to be.

Three

———

"**I** think I've just about got it," J.D. said confidently as he tinkered again with what he hoped Maggie regarded as a total mystery of machinery and mazes. If she knew any-thing—anything at all about engines—he had about as much of a chance of pulling this off as a rock had floating.

Though still fairly silent, she'd really been a sport. When he'd suggested an extra pair of hands would come in handy to hold a wrench while he tightened a few screws and oiled a few gears, she'd drawn a wary but determined breath and followed him to the plane.

It had been a cheap trick. But he wasn't above pulling it. Not when the result placed him in such deliciously close proximity to the spring-fresh scent of her hair and the summer-warm heat of her body. And she looked so damn cute with that smudge of grease on her nose.

He'd even gotten an exasperated grin out of her when he'd told her to put more pressure on the dowadidie so he could tighten the whatsitduger which in turn would make the thingamajigger work the way it was supposed to.

"Technie talk," he'd confided in a patronizing tone and a superior air that had finally won that smile.

It had been worth the wait. Though tempered with a worthy suspicion that told him he was going to have to keep on his toes or she'd find him out, he loved the look of her when she smiled. A certain sweetness hovered around the edges of that smile. A childlike vulnerability that he knew she'd never confess to. The wonder of it made his heart clench. The reason for it remained a mystery and the source of a dark and brooding concern.

"Okay," he said with staged hope as he retightened a screw he'd just loosened. "Let's see if that did the trick."

Wiping his hands on a rag, he closed the engine cowling with determined finality. "Kiss for luck?" he suggested with raised brows and a hopeful grin as he ripped off a fresh strip of duct tape and slapped it across the broken cowling latch to hold it closed.

She rolled her eyes, which made him laugh. Which made her scowl as she stepped back. He chose to interpret her scowl as reluctance at his imminent departure and was still grinning when he climbed into the cockpit.

"Come on sweetheart," he murmured, making a great show of coaxing and cajoling the engine. "Make daddy proud. I've got great expectations."

After a series of misfires and a bevy of sputters and *chuck-a-chucks*, the engine finally sparked, fired and hummed to life.

J.D. flashed Maggie a victorious smile, then throttled back to idling speed. Lord, he loved the look of her. She was trying to look relieved when, in fact, he figured she was fighting disappointment, which implied that she didn't want him to leave. Which, as far as he was concerned, more than justified the creative license he'd taken with his repairs.

With his grin still firmly in place, he crawled back out of the cockpit.

"We did it, Stretch," he yelled above the engine noise, then sidestepped Hershey when the lab made a flying leap for the shotgun seat.

They shared a soft smile at the dog's eagerness.

"Don't suppose you'd want to sign on as my ace mechanic?" He rose his brows hopefully.

"I think I'll leave that to you."

"What?" He moved closer, even though he'd heard every word. "I can't hear you. The noise," he yelled, angling a thumb back toward the plane as he lowered his head until his ear was a whisper away from her mouth.

"I said, I think I'll leave that to you!" she shouted.

"Aw, Stretch." He cupped her shoulders in his hands and gave her his most soulful look. "I don't want to leave you either!"

She shook her head vehemently. "No. That's not what I said!"

"You'd feel bad if I was dead?"

She rolled her eyes. "I don't believe this."

"A kiss? Jeez, Stretch. I thought you'd never ask."

She hadn't any more than opened her mouth to adamantly correct him when he lowered his head to hers.

There was something to be said for surprise attacks. Something to be said for a shocked, pliant woman and the sneak-up-on-you chill of a slow, creeping sunset that drew heat to heat, heartbeat to heartbeat.

J.D. folded her into his arms without restraint and savored the sweetness of her mouth, the softness of her body, the wonderful fit of her five-foot-ten stature to his mere four-inch advantage.

The lady thought this was goodbye. And once she figured out that this wasn't where the scene was going, she kissed like it was goodbye.

The wary tension seeped out of her limbs like frost melting on sun-warmed windowpanes. The reluctance to participate relaxed to a lazy acquiescence to the wonder of the moment and the richness of shared passions.

She molded her long length against his, held on like he was her anchor in a swirling sea of sensation and rode with him to the rise and fall of each deep, seductive swell.

It felt good. It felt like heaven. And ending it was one of the hardest things J.D. had ever done.

He pulled away slowly. His heart hammering. His emotions beating out a tune he was neither familiar with nor certain of. She felt it too. He could see it in her eyes. Sense it with each thready breath she drew. And as they stood there, the dusk fast descending and the urgency for his departure eminent, he saw a shadow of regret cloud her dark eyes.

A scene from an old war movie flicked across his mind's eye. He wasn't sure which movie. It didn't really matter. There was always a dramatic parting scene between the brave RAF pilot and his poignantly crying lover, a heroine of the French Resistance. The reluctant but resigned destiny of his call to duty darkened the hero's eyes; the silent but futile plea to stay glistened in hers.

"I gotta go, Stretch," he whispered as sappy sentiments blended sweetly with their own parting and he hoped for an invitation to stay.

No such luck. She crossed her arms beneath her breasts in that way he was beginning to recognize as an attempt to both create distance and provide self-protection.

He let out a deflated breath when she gave him a stiff nod, distancing herself even further. Guess he could rule out romance—but not a change of plans.

A lesser man would have counted on luck to stay his departure. He wasn't a lesser man.

When he'd pulled the fuel line earlier—with a fervent prayer she hadn't noticed or wouldn't realize what he'd done if she had—there had only been enough gas in the engine to run for a few minutes.

Though he was still stunned from the impact of their kiss and a little slow on the uptake, when the engine died on cue, he finally remembered to look shocked. He might have even managed to look a little disappointed.

What he felt was guilt. Okay, so only a little guilt, especially in light of the rewards he might reap because of his duplicity.

His slight hesitation cost him points, though. He caught a glimmer of suspicion in her eyes at the moment before he turned to the plane, gave the obligatory disgusted sigh and hung his hands dejectedly on his hips.

"Damn," he muttered, hoping he sounded convincing.

"Yeah," she echoed without an ounce of inflection in her voice. She narrowed her dark eyes and glared at him. "Damn."

Maggie smelled a rat the size of a whale—or in this case, the size of a very large, very blond Minnesotan.

She stared from his broad back to the plane.

"Problem?" she asked dryly.

"Could be," he said with a thoughtful frown. "Let me try her again."

But of course, when he climbed back into the pilot's seat, made all the appropriate adjustments and schooled his face into the picture of determination, the engine lay as quiet as the descent of the sun.

Something about the too, too dejected look on his face had her gritting her teeth.

Damn the man. Damn the man and his reckless grin and his sneak attacks and his potent kisses. And his stupid, worthless plane!

"Now what?" She didn't even try to hide her disgust.

"Well," he began, checking the dwindling daylight, "it's a cinch I can't get her running before dark. And even if I could, while I don't mind flying at night, I don't much like the idea of landing in the dark without ground or water lights. And I like the look of that cloud bank moving in even less.''

For the first time, Maggie noticed the darkening sky wasn't due only to the approaching sunset. A big thunderhead had moved in, black and threatening with the promise of rain and the potential of wind.

''So where's base?'' she asked on a resigned sigh.

''Crane Cove.''

One of the things Maggie had done when she'd moved into the cabin was acquaint herself fully with the lay of the lake. Crane Cove was less than an hour away by air. By land, however, they were looking at a four-hour trip. She didn't much care for the possibility of being cloistered in her Jeep with this man—no matter how charming—for that long. It would give him more than enough time to chip away at her resolve and make her want to confide in him.

''Can you radio someone to come pick you up?'' she suggested, searching for an alternative.

''Radio?''

She gave him a baleful look. ''Don't tell me you don't have a radio in the plane.''

''Yeah, well, sure. I've got a radio. But—''

''No,'' she cut in with a quelling scowl. ''Let me guess. It doesn't work.''

Again came that exasperating and irritatingly infectious grin. ''Got it in one, Stretch. Looks like you're stuck with Hershey and me for the night.''

She glared at him.

He had the nerve to laugh.

''I'll drive you back,'' she said with a single-minded determination to get rid of him.

''Oh, no you won't. I won't put you out that way. Besides, there's a stretch of road about ten miles long that's torn up. You'd need a Sherman tank to get through that mess. Especially if it rains," he added with a meaningful nod toward the sky.

She let out a deep, defeated breath.

"Hey," he said, cutting through thoughts that included murder and mayhem. "It's no sweat, okay? This is northern Minnesota. And you're looking at an outdoorsman. I'm *always* prepared for impromptu camp-outs. My tent is stowed in the Cessna. Hershey and I can pitch it in your front yard. We'll sleep under the clouds, stay warm by the camp fire and howl at the moon for entertainment. It'll be fine. It'll be great. You'll see. You'll forget we're even here."

Forget he was here? There was about as much chance of that as there was forgetting the way she'd reacted when he'd given her what she'd thought was a goodbye kiss. Something had happened to her in that moment. Something powerful and frightening and totally beyond her control.

She'd been swamped with an undeniable regret that he was actually going to leave her. As impossible as it seemed, she hadn't wanted him to go. And as he'd bent his head to hers, his intent as clear as the blue of his eyes, she'd told him as much, not with words, but with her body.

She'd molded herself against him, clung to him like scented lotion to sun-parched skin, melted like candle wax set to flame. And he'd answered her unspoken request to stay with a sweet seduction that had taken and indulged and promised a pleasure even greater if she'd just say the word.

She swallowed hard. Forget he was here? Not in this lifetime. That didn't mean he had to know it.

"Fine," she said crisply. "Camp on the lawn." Then, turning on legs bent on wobbling, she walked up to the cabin, determined to at least make him think she was capable of forgetting about him.

*   *   *

"Well, Hersh," J.D. groused as he settled into his sleeping bag and the lab curled up beside him, "looks like the lady took me literally. I think she did forget about us."

Maybe he shouldn't have been so enthusiastic when he'd assured her he'd be fine out in the elements. He hadn't thought at the time that he'd been all that convincing.

"Goes to show how much I know, huh, boy? Because I also figured she'd invite us in."

He cast a scowling glance toward the dark cabin. She'd walked away a little over three hours ago and he hadn't seen her since.

At the very least, he'd expected an offer to sleep on her couch. Hell, he'd have settled for the floor. Anything would have been softer than this rock his tent was pitched on.

He hit the button illuminating the dial on his watch. Only half an hour until midnight. It was going to be a long wait until morning. He'd built his fire for warmth but foregone cooking for the slices of summer sausage, cheese and crackers he'd packed in the little cooler he always carried in the plane. Hershey had been content with his dog chow and a couple of crackers. After a little recreational game of hide-and-seek with another chipmunk, the lab had settled in beside him.

"She's going to be a tougher nut to crack than I'd originally thought," J.D. reflected aloud as he turned on his back, made a final check of the black clouds rolling across the night sky and hoped for a tender heart in the event of rain. In absence of an invitation, he prayed that the hastily applied patches of duct tape he'd slapped across the new tears in his old tent would hold. He hated getting wet. Truth to tell, he hated camping out—though he'd never admit it aloud. Not to his friends, at any rate. They'd laugh him out of the state—especially if they found out that his idea of roughing it included a microwave and a CD player.

While he loved the north country, he loved it between sunrise and dusk, when the air was sweet and crisp and the sun was warm and mellow. By night, even in the summer, the lake land could be cold and sometimes dangerous. Shadows bled into shapes—many of them wild black bears, scavengers of the night, propelled to roam by boundless appetites that made them easy prey to the poachers currently plaguing the area.

Tomorrow would be soon enough to worry about them again. Tonight he had to worry about staying warm. And dry. When the sun had disappeared for the day, the warm breeze had shifted to a stout northwesterly, carrying a hint of an arctic chill. For a while the moon and the mosquitoes had been the only friendly company in the dark.

"I could do without the mosquitoes, but I wouldn't have minded a little more moonlight," he grumbled. The cloud bank had completely darkened the sky. "Wouldn't have minded a soft bed, either," he added grumpily as he tugged the sleeping bag higher over his shoulder and grudgingly accepted that it was going to be a long, cold night.

That was when he felt the first raindrop fall. A big splattering drop bulleted its way in through the trailing flaps of the pup tent, which were suddenly snapping like sheets in the wind.

He poked his head outside.

"Holy hurricane, Hersh!" He swore above the sudden and aggressive slap of the wind and rain pelting him full in the face. "Looks like we're in for a dam buster."

Hershey, ever the loyal companion, took one peek outside the tent, gave J.D. an every-dog-for-himself look and broke for the cabin. He was whining and scratching on the door—something J.D. was about ready to do himself—when he heard a screech of metal scraping against wood.

He snapped his attention toward the dock. With the rising wind came rising waves. The smoothly rolling surface of the bay had transformed in a heartbeat into a boiling cauldron of black water and crashing surf. And the Cessna, tied as she was to the end of the dock, was taking a hell of a beating against the cedar pilings that were anchored with re-rod stakes and rock.

J.D. didn't stop to think. He just reacted. He had to get her out of there or his beloved plane would end up a twisted, scattered mass of mangled metal and shattered glass.

Quickly slipping into his shoes, he made a mad dash for the end of the dock. In the next instant, he was on his knees, tugging at the ropes securing the plane, struggling with rain-soaked nylon and swearing into the wind when the knots wouldn't give.

By the time the first knot grudgingly slipped free, he was soaked to the skin. The icy wind and the force of the rain stung like tiny, piercing needles against his face. Ignoring the pain and cold, he scrambled to the front float. With concentrated effort and fingers rapidly stiffening and growing clumsy due to the cold, he freed the other rope.

Then and only then, did he allow himself enough time to make a decision. The Cessna was like a crippled bird with her fuel line pulled. He cursed himself for his "brilliant" maneuvering that made it impossible for him to crank her up and drive her to the safety of a sheltered harbor. If he simply let the plane go and the wind took her, she wouldn't stand much more of a chance of surviving intact than if he'd left her tied to the dock.

That left only one alternative. A brilliant flash of lightning lit up the night like a strobe, lighting the way to the beach thirty yards away. If he could tow the Cessna around the rocks to the beach, she could weather out the storm there without taking a battering. He could beach her on the sand and she'd sit as tight as a hen mallard on a nest, free from harm.

Thirty yards. Through a curtain of wind whipped rain, he gauged the angry breakers and the jutting ridge of massive boulders and jagged rock that lay between the dock and the beach. It might as well be thirty miles. On a deep breath, he considered the distance around the rock pile and the water's fifteen-foot depth, and the power of both to crush him.

Thirty yards of black, angry water and the very real probability that even if he survived the rock pile, he'd get sucked under and never come back up.

The Cessna cracked hard against the dock again, shaking the wood beneath his feet. When she bobbed up like a huge, gangly cork, he saw the damage. The tail end of a re-rod spike securing the cedar dock cribbing had gouged an angry-looking hole in one of the floats. It was then that he realized that if he stood there much longer debating, he'd lose her for good. When water filled the float, there was every possibility that she'd sink like a stone. And he simply couldn't let that happen.

Without another thought to his own safety, he peeled off his sweatshirt and toed off his shoes. Clutching the rope attached to the front float tightly in his fist, he sucked in a deep breath and took a running leap off the end of the dock.

Maggie had fooled herself into thinking she could sleep. Why she thought tonight would be different from any other, she didn't know. Insomnia had been her companion for several years, her persistent nemesis, always crowding her, always winning the battle of wills.

Tonight, with Blue Hazzard camped on her doorstep, it was a sure winner hands down.

She knew she had to concede that battle, but she wouldn't give up the other one. She would not invite him in. She would not let him and his every-mother-loves-him grin and his sneak-up-on-you sense of humor, or even her own tendency to mother stray dogs and feed alley cats, sway her.

Or the memory of his kiss.

A swift, sweet tug of arousal arched through her body, then settled heavy and low. It was bad enough that she'd let him kiss her. Even worse, she'd kissed him back. And she'd enjoyed it. She'd enjoyed the sure and sudden reawakening of desire, the honest ache of passion. She'd welcomed the reminder that she was a woman who could still be ruled by instincts that could so decisively eclipse her unbreachable control. At least she'd thought it was unbreachable.

Her relationship with Rolfe had taught her the power and necessity of control. A relationship with a man like Blue Hazzard could threaten, if not destroy it. And loss of control could end up destroying her.

That's why she couldn't let him any closer. That's why he couldn't sleep on her sofa. He might have stumbled on to her by accident, but the fact that he was still here was as calculated as her plan to drop out of life as she'd known it.

He'd set her up. She could feel it as certainly as she felt her fatigue fight with her inability to get a good night's sleep.

So she made herself stay in bed. Made herself quit getting up every five minutes to look out the window and see if the camp fire was still burning. Made herself stop trying to catch a glimpse of the sculpted angles of his profile as the firelight played across his features, tipping his golden hair with shades of amber and burnt sienna.

She willed herself to quit wondering if he was the kind of man he seemed to be. A man who loved life, loved to play, wasn't above a little good-natured manipulating to get what he wanted, but didn't have a mean bone in his body beneath all that sizzle and sex appeal.

No, she told herself firmly. Don't get caught up in wishing for the impossible. Don't get fooled by the pretty package. And for God's sake, don't forget what you're running away from.

She rolled to her stomach, determined to ride this out until tomorrow when he'd be gone. The first drop of rain pelted the bedroom window then. The unmistakable howl of a rising wind was quick to follow. The sharp scrape and whine at her door came soon after that.

She scowled into the pillow then assimilated the sound with the cause. Hershey.

Her nurturing heart ruled her actions then. Poor baby. The lab was scared. Maggie knew all about fear. The fear of being left alone. The fear of wondering where her next meal would come from. The fear of wondering if she'd ever find a safe haven.

She tossed back the covers and snagged her robe from a chair by the bed. Shivering with the chill of the Minnesota night, she tied the robe tightly around her waist and walked on bare feet to the living room.

When she opened the door, it was to the most pitiful sight she'd ever seen. Hershey sat, one paw up, his ears hanging low, his brown eyes big and soulful and pleading. And while his thick brown coat had shed the rain as effectively as duck down, he was shivering as if he'd been caught in an ice storm.

"You ought to take that show on the road," Maggie murmured with an amused shake of her head, then opened the door wide enough for the lab to snake through. "People would pay big money to see such a stellar performance— Hey! Where do you think you're going?"

Just that fast, Hershey, with the instincts of a coonhound, homed in on the bedroom, made one huge happy leap and landed in the middle of her bed. With a grunt of satisfaction, he nosed under the covers and burrowed deep.

"You little finagler," Maggie scolded as she trailed after the damp dog and tried to coax him out from under the blankets.

Hershey's only response was a low, warning growl.

Maggie grinned. "So you want to play hardball, huh?"

Hands on her hips, she stared at the lump in the middle of the mattress and wondered why she wasn't more upset. In the next instant, she knew the reason. Where the dog went, so went the man. So why hadn't he been begging at her door with Hershey?

An electrifying bolt of lightning cracked through the night, illuminating the dark cabin and the world outside the window.

She stood transfixed as her eyes took in the sudden storm, the violent crash of water to shore—and the figure hunched on his knees at the end of her dock.

Even through the dark and even at this distance, his size made it impossible to mistake him for anyone but Blue. Her brows drew together in instinctive alarm as she walked closer to the window. "What is he doing?"

Though her vision was hampered by darkness and rain-washed windowpanes, she didn't have to wonder long. Another lightning flash lit up the night just as he leaped into the bay.

"Oh, my God." One hand rose instinctively to her mouth while the other hugged her waist. "Is he crazy?"

For a full minute she stood there, trying to search him out amid the flashes of lightning and the black murky swells that battered her dock and crashed against the shoreline. When she saw a slow and gradual inching of the plane away from the dock, struggling to stay clear of the rocks, she understood.

He was trying to save the plane. That stupid, beat-up plane. And he was liable to drown himself or get fried by lightning in the process.

"Not only are you a conceited, arrogant jerk, you are certifiably insane, Blue Hazzard," she muttered under her breath. "And you're really going to get yourself killed this time."

For all of ten seconds she debated. Then she whipped off her robe, tugged on a pair of sweats over her panties and

T-shirt and jammed her feet into her tennis shoes. Snagging a flashlight from above the refrigerator, she grabbed her slicker from the coat rack and headed out the door.

Shoulders hunched against the downpour, she hurried down the slope toward the lake, rounded the boathouse, stopped, then backtracked. After finding a length of rope inside the boathouse, she headed back along the shoreline toward the beach. With every step she refused to think that he might have already drowned out there. With every stumble, she took solace in the fact that though the Cessna was not making much progress, she could still spot its silhouette bobbing wildly in the confines of this small finger of the bay. As long as the plane was inching its way toward the beach, that meant Blue was out there struggling. The damn fool! If he got out of this alive, she was going to cheerfully strangle him.

The beach was only thirty yards from the dock by water. By land, it was more like a hundred. She had to skirt an outcropping of rock, work her way carefully through a weaving uphill path through the woods and then, at the clearing, maneuver her way down a ten-foot cliff wall that gradually sloped to the small, protected cove with its sandy beach below.

In daylight and dry weather, the sandy gold beach was a pleasant little hike and a prize worth pursuing, a rarity in this glacial lake where shoreline was carved primarily from stone. In the dark, however, it was a slippery, treacherous trek. Uneven stones and gnarled tree roots grabbed at her toes and tried to trip her. Jagged rock and rain-slickened lichen made purchase hazardous and the going slow.

Finally, she reached the bottom of the rock wall, her ankles scratched, her shoes soggy, her hair flattened to her head and dripping over her eyes, blinding her.

She shoved it away from her face and ran to the edge of the sand. Fanning the flashlight's beam out into the water, she searched the rolling surface for a sign of Blue.

She'd weathered her share of wild, unexpected rainstorms in the past two months. Sometimes the skies turned heavy and gun metal gray in the hours before the rain came. Then it would settle in for days, the rain itself steady, the winds rising and falling with the tide. Sometimes, though, like tonight, the storms came with little or no warning. Screeching out of the night like a banshee, the wind would flex its muscle, turning the lake into a hazardous tumult of four- and five-foot swells that rolled over everything in its path.

Blue Hazzard was in its path right now—and it was battering him like a heavyweight going in for the knockout punch. She sucked in a harsh breath when she saw his head surface, then disappear when he was sucked into the belly of a swell that swallowed him completely.

"Blue!" She screamed his name above the wind's roar, then cried out in relief when he bobbed to the surface again.

"He'll never make it," she thought frantically, gauging the distance between him and the shore. Not with that damn plane in tow. And yet she knew he'd never let it go.

Fueled by anger as much as by fear for him, she planted the heel of the flashlight in the sand. The light beam arched upward like a beacon for him to follow. Then she searched for the nearest boulder. With the wind and icy rain slowing her down, she dropped to her knees in the sand and tied one end of the rope securely around it.

Rising to her feet and fighting the slicker that flapped against her legs and hampered her movements, she gripped the loop of rope and ran to the edge of the beach. With all her strength, she threw the loose end of the rope as far as she could toward the spot where she'd last spotted Blue.

The limp nylon barely made it ten yards before the wind sucked it down, stopping its outward arch. The coil of rope landed uselessly in the water several yards short of the mark. Her hopes of reaching him sank as the waves washed the floating tangle back to shore like sea foam.

With a deep, determined breath and a silent curse for her own poor judgment, she made a decision. If she was going to help him, she wasn't going to be able to do it from here.

She shrugged out of her slicker and stripped down to her panties and T-shirt. Shivering violently, she grasped the rope snugly in her hand. Setting her sights toward the nose of the Cessna, she waded into the hammering, icy surf toward the spot where she'd last seen Blue go under.

Four

J.D. had made some reckless decisions in his life. Diving into this churning lake at midnight might just top the list. But he'd do it again in a heartbeat if it meant the difference between saving or losing his plane.

When he saw the flash of light on the beach in a short, focused moment of clarity, however, he knew that this time he might have gone too far. This time it wasn't just his own safety that was being compromised.

Maggie. My, God! She must have seen him out here, figured he was in trouble and decided to come in after him.

"No!" he yelled around a mouthful of lake water as a vicious undertow yanked him beneath the surface again with the zealous strength of a possessive lover.

Muscling his way to the surface, he broke the crest of a wave spitting water and gulping for air. "Maggie—g-go back!"

The screaming wind stole his water-choked words, whipping them back into the midst of the storm and out of her earshot.

"Go back!" he yelled again as she stumbled and went down fifteen yards ahead of him.

He lost sight of her completely then. And in that moment, he discovered fear as he'd never known it. Heart-stalling, chest-crushing, forget-to-breathe fear. His lungs burned. His ribs ached with each wild, laborious lurch of his heart as he searched the undulating surface and swore at the undertow that was determined to suck him out into open water and away from Maggie and the beach.

"Maggie!" he roared. He was desperate to find her, determined that he would, or die trying. It came down to saving her or the plane. Without a second thought, he let go of the tow rope and dove for her.

Cold, murky blackness—so thick it made his lungs contract, so heavy it felt like his eardrums would burst—blocked his way. He groped blindly for a connection—any connection—with an arm or a leg or, please, God, a handful of that glorious chestnut hair.

When he could stand it no longer, he broke to the surface, sucking air, stalling panic. Clinging to the necessity of a clear head, he dragged in another lung full of air and was ready to go under again when he heard her voice.

"Hazzard!"

Through a vortex of funneling wind and pounding waves, it came to him. The sweetest sound. The truest tone. The proof that he hadn't lost her to the lake. He whipped around toward the sound that was now behind him, straining to see through the darkness.

"Maggie!" he swore, disbelieving when he spotted her, only her head and the slope of her shoulders visible above the aggressive surf.

"Grab—grab the rope!" she yelled, fighting to be heard above the wind and the crash of water to rock. "The rope!" she repeated in a frazzled, frustrated command. "Grab it!"

Only then did he realize she'd strung a lifeline from the shore to the spot where she treaded water. And only then did he realize she held it in one hand, and the Cessna's rope was in her other hand.

With a whoop of jubilation and relief he dove for her. "You sweet, stupid woman! What the hell do you think you're doing?" he demanded when he reached her. Wrapping her snugly in his arms, he lifted her above the choppy surface.

"I'm saving your worthless neck!"

Spitting water and trying, unsuccessfully, to rake the soaked tangle of knotted hair from her face, she let him relieve her of the weight of the Cessna's rope as the waves fought to lure the plane out to open water.

"Damn right you are!" Rain pelted him in the face as he laughed into her eyes. "And you saved my plane, too! When we get out of here, lady, I'll show you just how grateful I am." Lightning cracked across the night sky. "But you gotta get out of this water, Maggie. Now!"

He turned her around and shoved her none too gently ahead of him toward the beach. "Get the hell back to shore!" he demanded, making sure she had a death grip on the lifeline. "That lightning is too damn close.

"Go!" he ordered as he fought with the tow rope and she hesitated, determined to help him.

With a scowl as dark as the night, she finally obeyed. She worked her way slowly along the rope as the water and the wind combined in an attack force against her. Only when she was well on her way did J.D. tie the ends of the two ropes together, securing the safety of the plane. And only when he was sure his knot was fast did he follow her, fighting his way by inches, to the beach.

Drained and winded, he crawled the last yard to the shore on hands and knees and collapsed face first in the surf-soaked sand.

Beside him, prostrate and exhausted, Maggie lay like a limp rag doll, her breath coming in labored, gasping gulps.

With the last of his strength, J.D. rolled toward her. Gathering her in his arms, he sheltered her against the wind and rain that pummeled them both.

"Are you all right?" he demanded, raking the tangled snarl of wet hair away from her eyes.

She nodded and burrowed closer to his heat.

"God, Maggie." He lowered his mouth to her hair. "You scared ten years off my life. If... if anything had happened to you, I'd never be able to live with myself."

He drew her closer still, shaken by the violent trembling of her body, taken by her valor, seduced by her near-naked wet length. And there, with the wind and the rain cocooning them like shipwrecked survivors, the romantic in him eclipsed his concern and his current discomfort.

She was a quivering bundle of lush feminine flesh. Near naked. Near freezing. Nearly his for the taking.

Her soaked T-shirt had ridden up high on her hip, exposing a strip of delicate white silk banded together by tiny ribbons of lace at her hip point. The soft fullness of her breasts with their diamond-hard nipples pressed against him, separated from his bare chest by the mere barrier of clinging, wet cotton. Another movie scene came vividly to mind, this one a foreshadowing of everything he wanted to share with Maggie—the heat, the passion, the desperate need:

A man and a woman lay entwined in each other's arms on a remote, moon-lit beach. Not just any man. Not just any woman. Burt Lancaster and Deborah Kerr rolled in the surf-swept sand, oblivious to the crash of the breakers around them, locked in each other's arms, lost in each other's love....

"Blue..."

"Yes, Maggie," he whispered, closing his eyes, letting himself get swept up in the moment and the miracle as it unfolded.

"Blue...if you don't get your grubby paws off of me, my knee is going to connect with a part of your anatomy that *you*, no doubt, highly value, and that *I* could happily put out of commission for the rest of your natural life."

His eyes snapped open. He pulled back, blinked, then blinked again. "Huh?"

"Back off, buster," she gritted out between chattering teeth.

"Oh." Reality interloped on fantasy with grating finality. "Oh, yeah. I'm...ah, sorry. Can...can you, ah, get up?"

She glared at him. "I could if you'd get off me."

"Oh. Ah, yeah. Sure."

He wasn't quite sure when he'd been reduced to monosyllabic mutterings. Somewhere between here and eternity he'd guess—or between the mention of her knee and his highly valued parts. The look in her eyes warned him that she meant business. Since he had plans for those parts that included both him and her, instinct took over.

With a strength he hadn't thought was left in him, he sprang to his feet. As an afterthought, he offered her his hand.

She didn't just ignore it. She made a great show of looking at his outstretched hand, then glaring at him as if to say, "I wouldn't accept your help if you were the last degenerate on earth."

She rose to her feet on her own steam. Without a word, she gathered her soaked clothes in her arms and headed up the stone cliff.

Halfway up the slope, she turned back to him. "Hershey, at least, was smart enough to come in out of the rain. If you can muster up a fraction of his intelligence, you can do the same. That is, if you don't strain something dragging that damn plane to shore.''

While her words were harsh and judgmental, the look in her eyes gave him hope. She may be mad—okay, so she was livid—but she was also concerned about him. Just when he'd thought all was lost. She cared, bless her. She didn't want to but she did.

Even the glare she leveled at him before she turned and began making her way along the slope didn't fool him. Katharine Hepburn always gave Spencer Tracy that look—just before she threw herself into his arms and told the big lug she loved him.

"Everything was so simple yesterday," Maggie muttered under her breath as she lifted the whistling teakettle off the stove and filled two mugs with boiling water. "I was alone. I was in peace. I was not up at two in the morning with a seventy-pound ball of fur hogging my bed and a two-hundred-twenty-pound drowned rat occupying my shower.''

She tried not to be concerned about Blue while she stood in the kitchen and he stood in the bathroom under a hot shower trying to coax some warmth back into his bones. But he'd been out in the storm a lot longer than she had and she'd felt awful by the time she finally made her way back to the cabin. She'd been cold to the point of brittle, her joints aching, her fingers and toes stinging and her teeth chattering so hard she'd managed to bite her tongue.

A long, hot shower had helped her. So had the fire she'd laid in the little wood stove—as she'd done every night in the event she needed to take the chill off the cabin. She sent a silent prayer of thanks toward whatever power had sent her Abel Greene two months ago. He'd just shown up out of nowhere that day she'd arrived, and in addition to helping her open up the cabin and making some minor repairs to the place, Abel had taken to checking on her at regular intervals and seeing to it that her wood pile was well stocked.

Unlike Blue Hazzard, who had been nothing but a pain, Abel Greene had been a gift. Like Blue, Abel was a big man. Big, uniquely beautiful, and at first meeting imposing. The first time she'd seen him emerge from the woods looking for all the world like an untamed and savage warrior with his long black hair flowing down his back and his silver-eyed wolf dog by his side, she'd almost packed up and headed back to civilization. She'd gotten used to Abel's unannounced visits since then. And to his silent stoicism.

Abel was an enigma she had given up trying to figure out. That was her gift to him. She didn't pry. Didn't prod. She accepted that what he gave her was also satisfying some need of his own. And she recognized the wounded spirit inside him. She recognized it because it was so like her own.

A crash of thunder rattled the windows, making her jump. The storm had not lessened in intensity. If anything, it had gotten worse.

Dressed in dry sweats and heavy socks with a towel wrapped turban style over her hair, she gathered all three oil lamps she'd discovered in the cabin in preparation for the loss of electricity that seemed inevitable.

That done, she settled into the worn sofa with her mug of hot cocoa and a warm blanket, and waited for Blue to join her there. That, too, seemed inevitable. After all, she couldn't very well refuse him the comfort of a fire—even though a firing squad was more to her liking.

He'd followed her to the cabin a full half hour after she'd left him on the beach. When he'd finally rapped on her back door, his lips had been as blue as his eyes. She didn't have to ask what had taken him so long. He'd been beaching the Cessna. Putting his precious baby to bed.

She'd shoved a dry towel into his shaking hands, pointed him toward the shower and shut the bathroom door.

Staring thoughtfully into the fire, she turned out the sounds of the storm outside and grudgingly admired him for his devotion—even though she thought he was a fool for risking his neck like that. Wistfully, she wondered what it would be like to have someone care about her as much as Blue cared about his plane. Foolishly, she wondered what it would be like if that someone was Blue.

The bathroom door opened just in time to quell that dangerous thought. With concentrated effort, she schooled her attention and her eyes to remain on the fire.

It was a temporary respite at best. Avoiding him would be impossible. Although the little log cabin in the woods had all the basic amenities of electricity and indoor plumbing, square footage was not its greatest asset. The single bedroom and bathroom were the only rooms with doors. The kitchen-living area made up the bulk of the floor plan, open by design cozy by intent and close by proximity.

The wood stove sat in the corner of the knotty-pine paneled great room, nestled in the mortared lake-rock portion of the walls and sitting on a hearth of the same rock. The furniture—sturdy pine frames with upholstery of hunter's plaid—was arranged to face both the fire and the picture window and gave a postcard view of the bay by daylight, and an eye-of-the-storm sensation on a night like this.

"Is this for me?"

She looked up at the sound of Blue's voice to find him standing by the kitchen counter, looking hopefully at the mug of hot chocolate she'd left for him there.

All of her resolve to remain distant melted like the marshmallows floating in her mug when she met his blue-eyed smile and the obvious embarrassment he was trying to hide as he stood there in her pink chenille robe.

She couldn't help it. She smiled. Then she laughed. Giggled, actually. It just slipped out, a little rusty from lack of use, a little surprising in the ease with which it had escaped at the sight of his very huge self in her very small robe.

"You find this funny?" he said, deadpan, when she'd spent herself. "Fine. But I just want you to know that mini has never been my size. And pink has never been my color."

She sniffed and buried her nose in her mug to quell another chuckle. "Oh, I don't know. I think you look kind of pretty in pink."

They shared a grin then. How could she not smile at six feet two inches of testosterone packed into a robe made with estrogen in mind? Where the robe covered Maggie from chin to knee, it strained at the seams to hit him from midthigh to elbow, and wasn't having much luck at either. That wasn't even mentioning the bare expanse of muscled chest and, um, other things that threatened to peek out.

"Sorry I couldn't come up with something better. But until your clothes are dry, it's the best I could do."

Holding his cocoa in one hand and the robe closed with the other, he walked in front of her, then settled into the opposite end of the sofa.

"Could be worse," he said, stalling a shiver and snagging the extra blanket she'd laid out for him. With a mischievous glint in his eye, he raised his arm and sniffed the fabric of the robe that held the scent of the lotion she wore. "I can't remember when I've ever smelled this good."

They shared another sneak-up-on-you smile and she wondered when they had started coming so freely. Just like she wondered how a man in a woman's pink robe could look so undeniably sexy.

His hair was still damp from his shower. His only attempt at taming its wild disarray had been a quick finger combing that had somehow managed to arrange it with an artfulness that no stylist's brush could ever have achieved.

Everywhere the robe didn't cover—and that encompassed a lot of territory—the firelight gilded the summer bronze tint of his skin, set flickering highlights to the soft curling hair on his chest, defined the strong angles of his face with shadows and substance. His eyes were so blue, so intense, as they met hers above the rim of his mug.

She looked quickly away, embarrassed that he'd caught her staring, and cataloging, and wondering what it would be like to be made love to by Blue Hazzard.

That thought stopped her cold. Unsettling as it was, even more upsetting was the very real possibility that he could tell exactly what was running through her mind.

She'd been told for years that one of her most valuable assets was her ability to relay a gamut of emotions with nothing more than a look. She'd made her fortune on her face and the openness of the feelings she could express there. And she'd be a fool if she thought Blue hadn't known what she'd been thinking as she'd watched him.

She waited for him to call her on it, to push the advantage of a storm-drenched night, a warm fire and the vulnerability of a lonely woman. When he didn't, she couldn't help but meet his eyes again and question why.

He answered her silent query with a soft, easy smile and a deep sigh before he angled his gaze thoughtfully toward the fire.

"I owe you an apology, Stretch," he said into a silence broken only by the rush of the wind, the persistent peppering of rain on the windowpanes and the crackle of the cedar fire. "I put you at risk tonight."

She tucked her feet up under her bottom and arranged the blanket more snugly around her. "I was never at risk. And you didn't ask me to come after you. I made that decision myself."

"Yeah," he said, after a thoughtful silence, his deep voice pensive. "You did, didn't you. I guess the question is, why?"

She could feel his warm gaze touch her face, puzzled, pleased, liking the conclusions he'd drawn before ever hearing her reply.

"Well it wasn't like I could sleep or anything," she said, shooting for a disgruntled demeanor. "Not with your dog shivering under the covers of my bed and you bobbing around like a cork in my bay."

One corner of his mouth tipped up in a crooked smile. "Hersh does like his creature comforts."

"And you like to prove you're still the same reckless show-off you were fifteen years ago."

She tried to sound disgusted but it didn't come out that way. It came out sounding wistful instead, crowded with old memories that, if she let herself, she could find both comfortable and amusing.

"Yeah, well, I was in love. A man will do almost anything when he's in love."

"You weren't a man. And you weren't in love," she corrected him, and gave in to the recurring urge to smile as she tugged the towel from her hair. "You were an obnoxious pain in the neck locked in hormonal overload. And if I recall, I saved your sorry self once back then, too."

"Well, at least I let you *think* you did."

She angled him a suspicious look, stilling the hand she'd been working through her hair to fluff and dry it. "You mean you really didn't have a cramp that day I dove into the bay after you?"

He grinned sweetly. Angels should look so innocent.

"You toad," she sputtered, grudgingly accepting that he'd duped her all those years ago.

"Sorry," he said, without one speck of remorse. "But a guy had to do what a guy had to do. And it was heaven." He exhaled on a wistful sigh. "There I was—tucked safely in your arms as you swam me back to shore." He caught the towel she threw at him, chuckled and let his head fall lazily back against the sofa cushion. "And the mouth-to-mouth, well, I almost embarrassed myself over that."

"You really were a jerk, Hazzard," she said, but with a fondness in her voice that undercut her exasperation.

He let his head loll to the side, toward her. His gaze sought hers, the intensity in his eyes heightened by firelight and lightning flashes. "And you really were a beauty. Still are." He paused, genuine regret darkening his eyes again. "But even though I'd still try just about anything to get close to you, I'd never intentionally hurt you. I never meant for you to go out in that tonight."

"I know," she said, turning way, uncomfortable with his intentions, certain of his sincerity. "I'm fine. Nothing was hurt, okay?"

He grunted. "Nothing but my image. And maybe my pride."

"Ah, well. Time has managed to dispel the 'real men don't eat quiche' stigma. Maybe we'll break the pink bathrobe barrier soon, too."

He smiled crookedly and resumed his study of the fire.

"So, did you get warmed up?"

He took a careful sip of his hot cocoa. "Working on it."

"And the plane? Is it all right?" she asked rather than let the silence infuse them again with intimate thoughts and impossible options.

"She will be. She took a nasty gouge in the right float before I got her beached, but she'll ride out the storm okay where she is."

"Far be it from me to question your priorities, but why is that wreck so important to you?"

His eyes filled with affection and pride. "Remember Hank Townsend?"

She furrowed her brow but shook her head when she couldn't connect with the name.

"Old Hank was just about the best walleye guide between the Cities and Alaska. He was also one of the nicest old guys and one of the biggest characters I'd ever met. The first time I was ever airborne it was with Hank in that plane. It was that flight that turned me on to flying. And that little plane that gave me my first thrill."

He paused. A shadow of regret darkened his face. "When I heard that Hank had died a few years back, I made a trip up from the Cities to pay my respects to his kids and ended up buying the plane from them. She and I have been together ever since."

There was a certain sweetness about him as he told her the story. An innocence of spirit and purity of heart that tugged at feelings deep inside. Feelings she'd thought she'd lost and would be better off without, she told herself grimly, just as the lights went out.

"I've been waiting for that," she said, making to rise from the sofa and light the lamps.

A hand on her shoulder stayed her.

"Stay put," he said softly. "We don't need the lamps. The fire glow works for me."

It was working for her, too—too well. The dancing flames lent a subtle intimacy to a moment that eclipsed even the isolation inherent in the romantic scenario of one woman and one man alone in a cabin in the woods.

Even so, she let him coax her to settle back onto the sofa. "You mentioned the Cities. Were you living there then?" she asked, not, she told herself, because she was interested in his life, but to establish a definitive line between intimacy and necessity. It was a necessity to not court intimacy. It was a necessity to keep the conversation generic.

"I still do." He slouched lower on the sofa and stretched his long bare feet closer toward the warmth of the fire. "My business is there. Air cargo," he added in anticipation of her next question.

"Air cargo?"

"Yup. And actually, Minneapolis is basically headquarters now. Hazzard Aire is flying out of a dozen different cities at last count."

She tilted her head. "So he's a successful businessman."

He shrugged. "I've been lucky."

Maggie doubted that luck had much to do with it. Not in today's competitive business world. "You just happened to be up here on vacation?"

He smiled. "I've got competent people working for me so I leave the business in their hands and spend my summers up here."

Successful and smart, she concluded. Here was a man who was not going to let his life be consumed by corporate stress and an insatiable need to control the pulse of every aspect of his business. She should be so together, she thought ruefully, then reacted to the warmth in his eyes.

"So the lake got in your blood, too," she said with a speculative tilt of her head.

"Oh, yeah," he said, settling even lower on the couch and, if possible, stretching out a little longer as he propped his mug on his chest. He looked comfy and content and too, too appealing. "This place does that. There are memories here that never quite let go. And some traditions just refuse to die. My dad started bringing me to the lake when I was five years old. I've never spent a summer since without making some kind of an appearance. Even if it was only for a long weekend or two in those early days when I was getting the business off the ground—no pun intended.

"You probably won't believe this," he added in a voice softened by self-deprecation, "but I never gave up hope that I'd find you up here again."

He turned his head lazily on the sofa cushion, his gaze seeking hers in the firelight. "I've never spent a summer like the one I spent chasing you."

Maggie thought back to that summer. That wonderful, special time in her life when Max and Esther Snyder had made her feel cared for and cherished and loved. It had been a rarity in her life that had seen her shuffled from one foster home to another, from group home to group home in Chicago's inner city to a couple of ugly brushes with juvenile detention.

"You know, I've looked for you up here every year since then, Stretch."

His voice broke through her musings. Deep, compelling, so tempting with its knowledge of the feisty, streetwise girl she'd been, so forbidden because of his lack of insight about the apprehensive, distrustful woman she'd become.

"Somehow, I doubt that," she said, determined to diffuse the recurring threat of intimacy his straightforward admission fostered.

He didn't dispute her. Not in words. It was his silence, instead, that compelled her to look at him. *If it makes you feel better, doubt away,* his intense blue eyes and indulgent shrug suggested, *but I'm telling it straight.*

In her heart, she believed him. Her heart, it seemed, might just be leading her into trouble.

"It wasn't in the cards for me to come back," she said, determined to find her way back to safer ground.

"And yet you ended up here now."

How, Maggie? Why? Again, he didn't put voice to his questions. She heard them just the same. And in that moment, when his gaze searched hers with more interest and concern than anyone had lavished on her in more years than she cared to remember, she almost weakened and told him about Rolfe and how he had nearly destroyed her.

Almost. Her dependence might have slowed down her escape, but she hadn't gotten this far being weak. And she wouldn't get where she needed to go if she gave in to weakness now. Stubbornly, she sipped her hot chocolate, stared into the fire and hoped he'd consider the subject closed.

"I'd heard that the Snyders passed on." The gentle hesitance of his tone filled a silence that had expanded, rivaling the darkness for space in the cabin. "I'm sorry. It must have been hard for you to lose your grandparents."

She nodded and, feeling safer with the warm memories and tender sentiments that thoughts of the Snyders prompted, let go of a little bit of herself. "Yes, it was hard. As hard as if they'd really been a family.

"They were my foster grandparents," she clarified, answering the question in his eyes. "And they were two of the most special people I've ever known."

She stared into the fire. The memories brought a sudden mist to her eyes and clutched at the deepest center of her heart as she thought of the Snyders and the gift of love they'd given her.

When the news of their death had reached her two years ago, she'd felt like the only tie she'd had with security, however distant, had been broken. She'd only spent one summer with them. One magical, memorable summer with those two special people who had volunteered for the foster grandparents program and taken her into their home and their hearts.

She'd known her bond with them had been true, but she hadn't known how true until she'd grieved for them at their funeral, then wondered at their generous bequest.

In the same quiet way they had gone about making her feel she had worth and value, they had arranged for the cabin to be hers when they were gone.

Because you blossomed there, the simple note they'd left her said. *Because you were loved there.*

She'd mourned for the Snyders in secret. Just as she'd kept their bequest a secret along with her plans to escape to the cabin in the woods. Even in death, they had provided her with a safe haven.

No one could find her here. No one knew she was here. No one but Blue Hazzard.

Her gaze snapped back to his as a belated panic suddenly outdistanced her melancholy mood.

"I'd appreciate it," she began, choosing her words carefully, "if when you leave tomorrow that you don't tell anyone about me being here. If... if the press got wind of the cabin, I'd never be able to use it as a getaway again.

They'd be hanging in the trees trying to get shots of everything from my dirty dishes to my garbage."

Loss of privacy wasn't her only threat from the press. If they found her, Rolfe would, too. He'd come after her before she was strong enough to face him.

The dark look that came over Blue's face had her mentally kicking herself. Her explanation of why she wanted to avoid the press had been unnecessary. She was trying too hard and he knew it. He'd read more than annoyance in her eyes when she talked about invasion of privacy. He'd picked up on her fear. His frown told her he was wondering what caused it.

"You will keep my little secret, won't you, Blue?" she pressed on anyway, determined to extract a promise from this man who had already proven to her that if he made a promise, he kept it. Even if it was as fanciful as keeping a promise to himself that he would kiss her after all these years.

A long moment passed as their eyes met and held. "A lady's secret is always safe with me," he assured her with a soft smile that did little to hide his curiosity and concern. "Especially if the lady happens to be you, Stretch. Remember that," he added with an edgy emphasis he proceeded to drive home. "You can count on me. Anytime. For anything . . . anything you would ever need."

The relief she felt was like dead weight lifted from her chest. She drew a deep breath, thanking him with her eyes because she didn't think she was capable of speaking. She hadn't thought she was capable of moving either until he set his mug aside and leaned toward her.

"I'm your man, Maggie." He touched his hand to her face. "Whatever the need. Whatever the reason."

His eyes had turned a smoky indigo, like a shimmering midnight sky as he held her gaze, mesmerizing, tantalizing, promising things she yearned to believe in, offering things she dared not indulge in.

He was so close she could see the pulse beat at his throat, steady, strong, vital. He was so tempting, as the warmth of his callused hand caressed her face and he lowered his head to hers, that she couldn't make herself pull away.

She wanted more than life to give in to it all, to the pleasure he promised, to the safe harbor she'd been seeking her entire life. She tipped her head to the sheltering warmth of his palm, closed her eyes in anticipation of his kiss, then bolted like a deer in the sights of a hunter when lightning sizzled across the sky and a crack of thunder burst into the silence like a rifle shot of warning.

Her eyes snapped open in tandem with a heartbeat that leaped to her throat. She shot off the sofa, eyes wide and wary, arms wrapped protectively around her waist. She swallowed hard, working, working at catching her breath, working, working at regaining her equilibrium.

This couldn't happen. She couldn't let it. She didn't need it. She couldn't give in to the wants his kisses fostered. Couldn't expose herself to that kind of dependence again.

With a darting glance that she prayed wasn't as wild as the rapid-fire beat of her heart, she turned away from him. Without a word to explain her action, she hurried to her bedroom, shooed a disgruntled Hershey out of her bed and shut the door soundly behind her.

Hours passed before she slept. Hours of restless yearning that argued with common sense and made a shambles of her resolve. She lay in the dark and prayed he wouldn't come to her door. Then she'd pray that he would. That he'd taken the responsibility out of her hands by taking her, without asking, without hesitation.

Shamed, she buried her face in the pillow and hated herself for nearly succumbing again to the weakness that Rolfe had always used against her and that she seemed unable to control.

All she'd ever wanted was for someone to love her. It didn't seem so much to ask that someone felt a need to protect her, to care for her. To drive away the inner voices that had jeered and sneered at her since she was a child, ravaging her sense of self-worth, convincing her she wasn't worth the effort. At a very early age, experience had shown her she wasn't worth loving, wasn't worth cherishing, wasn't worth anything as a person. Only as a personality. Only as an object.

Blue Hazzard made her want to stand up to those voices that had taunted her forever. Blue Hazzard made her want to discount that her own mother hadn't wanted her. That a series of well-intentioned foster parents hadn't cared enough about her to make their arrangement permanent. He made her want to forget that Rolfe Sebastion, the man she'd thought loved her for what she was, had only been in love with her face and her body and the manipulative pleasure and profit he could gain from both.

She rarely gave in to the pain. Rarely let herself indulge in the selfishness of self-pity. Tonight she had no choice. It overwhelmed her like the storm. It surrounded her like the darkness. And only her fear of yet another rejection kept her from running straight to the man who could, for tonight at least, subdue and slay the beast that prowled so close to the edge of her northwoods sanctuary.

Five

The storm had blown itself out by morning. J.D. awoke to sunshine on his face, the orange red embers of last night's fire in the grate and Hershey crowding him off the sofa. Though Maggie was at the center of his thoughts, she was nowhere in sight.

Last night she'd been a bewitching assemblage of soft, wistful sighs and slow, tentative gazes underscored by sexual awareness and faraway looks containing sadness and pain.

He rubbed the sleep from his eyes and stared hard at the ceiling. Something was very wrong in her life. He was convinced of it. No matter how valiantly she tried to hide it, she didn't stand a chance of masking her true feelings. Not with that face. That beautiful, tragically sad face that projected every emotion she owned. She'd lose the farm in a poker game. Just like she'd almost lost her resolve last night—to keep whatever it was that was eating at her a secret from him.

The cabin had provided them with more than protection from the storm. It had cast them together, isolated them from the rest of the world. They'd settled into an easy intimacy that had encouraged confidence and trust—until he'd blown it by giving into his need to kiss her and that hunted look had returned to her eyes before she'd run away. But not before she'd extracted a promise that he keep her presence a secret.

As if he needed a reason to keep her to himself, he thought, remembering the feel of her cheek against the back of his knuckles when he'd finally worked up the nerve to reach out to her. He'd been about ready to tell her that— hell, he'd been ready to show her—when she'd shot off the sofa like someone had lit a stick of dynamite beneath her.

He sat up and plowed his fingers through his hair. The niggling concern about what had put that fear in her eyes had eaten at him all night. Her tight-lipped silence about it made him madder than blue blazes. It also drove home the fact that among the feelings she had awakened in him, this sense of responsibility was as strong as the tide and just as mysterious.

He wasn't a believer in karma or kismet or any of that transcendental hooey, but he wasn't prepared to blow off the possibility that their chance meeting after all these years had happened for a reason. He'd followed her career. His air cargo business took him all over the world—frequently to New York. He could have approached her a number of times. Yet he'd held off. He only realized now—now that he was with her again—that what he'd told her earlier was true. He really had been waiting for her to return to the lake where they'd first met.

And she'd come back. After fifteen years. There had to be some significance to that. And there had to be a reason.

Whatever it was, he wasn't fool enough not to take advantage of the opportunity life had handed him on a golden platter. She was here. They were together. He intended to keep it that way.

The problem was that if she kept shutting him out with forced silences and hurried getaways, he'd never find out if this was supposed to lead anywhere.

"Scooch over, you sofa slug," he grumbled when Hershey took advantage of his shift of position to stretch out full length across the cushions.

Hershey just moaned in doggy ecstasy and wriggled onto his back.

J.D. rolled his eyes and made room. "Your trouble is, you don't know who the dog is in the duo," he muttered, giving the lab the belly rubbing he was begging for.

"And my trouble," he said, tugging a blanket from under him and wrapping it around his hips as he stood up, "is solving Miss Maggie Adams' problem, then figuring if I'm going to be a factor in her life."

Tucking either end of the blanket securely around his waist, he laid some kindling on the embers and set to work coaxing the fire back to life. Though the day promised sunshine and July heat, the cabin held the lingering chill of last night's storm at this early hour.

He glanced at his watch, surprised to see it was already a little after seven. After loading the stove with wood, he rummaged around quietly in her cupboard, searching for something to secure the blanket before he bared it all to God and the rest of the free world.

"A woman after my own heart," he murmured with a pleased grin when he found a roll of duct tape tucked in the back of the cupboard. After tearing off a strip and taping the blanket around his hips, he craned his neck around to get a glimpse of the bedroom door. Seeing it open, he skirted the pine dinette set, padded barefoot across the worn puncheon floor and peeked inside.

The bed was made and the woman was gone. He hadn't any more than let that thought settle when footsteps announced her approach at the back door.

"Well, aren't you the early bird," he said, swinging open the door—and connecting squarely with the glacial stare of eyes as black as midnight—belonging not to Maggie but to a man as big and as unyielding as a mountain.

Abel Greene topped J.D.'s six-two by a couple of inches, outweighed him by possibly twenty lean pounds of muscle. In attitude, he also had J.D. beat by a country mile.

His long black hair, which was held back from his face with a dark blue bandanna, added to the drama and the intensity of his predatory glare and supported the story that he was a descendent of a French fur trader and a Chippewa maiden. And J.D. was *not* happy to see him at Maggie's door.

"What the hell are you doing here, Greene?"

Abel Greene stared back at J.D. with a stone-hard expression that relayed neither intimidation nor compromise. It was Greene's unreadable facade of impenetrable indifference that had earned him a reputation as an unfeeling loner and had made him the subject of speculation around the lake for years. Behind his back, he was also the target of a guarded ridicule that masked unease about the enigma he'd become.

J.D. had shared the speculation, but not the ridicule. His inclination, based on his few encounters with Greene, leaned more toward healthy respect and justifiable curiosity. Unfortunately, though, because of Greene's proximity to the black bear population around the lake area, J.D. was also reluctantly forced to accept the Department of Natural Resources' theory that Greene might be involved in the poaching ring.

The question of the moment, however, was what was the big man doing at Maggie's door.

"I said, what are you doing here, Greene?"

Greene answered with a question of his own. "Where's Maggie?"

More demand than query rang in Greene's words. Liking neither his attitude nor the implication that he had a right to ask about Maggie, J.D. crossed his arms over his chest and deepened his scowl.

His attention shifted abruptly when the dog by Greene's side—a dog the size of a small pony with the look and demeanor of a wolf—began to whine and scratch at the door.

"Nashata, quiet." Greene's short, soft command was nonnegotiable. The dog settled, sat, then stood again, her long tail tucked between her legs, slowly wagging as Hershey bounded off the sofa to investigate.

While the dogs pressed their noses to the screen to sniff and size up each other, J.D. and Greene did the human equivalent.

J.D.'s gaze was drawn to the angry-looking scar that ran the length of Greene's face from temple to jaw. Word had it a bear was responsible for that scar. It added to Greene's mystique and the hard fact that Greene could never be mistaken as anything but formidable.

Neither could J.D. mistake the fact that he and Maggie knew each other. He didn't much like that conclusion. And when Greene turned to the sound of approaching footsteps, J.D. didn't much like the way his features relaxed and the wolf dog left his side to accept, without hesitation, a pat from Maggie's hand.

Dressed in no-nonsense gray sweats, well-used running shoes and a sheen of perspiration that beaded on her flushed face, Maggie walked past the dog to Abel's side.

"My, my," she said, her speech stilted by the obvious fact that she was winded from a recent run, "seems there's no end to my unexpected visitors these days."

She gave Abel a reassuring smile. J.D. felt something clench in his gut like a vise grip. Just once, he'd like to see that kind of trust relayed in a look she gave him. Just that fast, he was determined he'd see that look directed at him. Soon.

"What brings you by this morning, Abel?" she asked as she raked the hair back from her face with her fingers, then dragged her forearm across her brow to wipe away the perspiration.

"It was a bad storm," he said in a voice made gravelly by lack of use, made deep by restrained concern. "Thought you might have had some trouble." His gaze swung meaningfully back to J.D.

"No trouble," J.D. said, opening the screen door and stepping outside. "At least not for the lady."

Hershey slipped out behind him. After gingerly approaching the wolf dog, he sniffed happily, woofed a friendly greeting, then bounded into the woods for a morning romp. The wolf dog waited for a nod from Greene before she followed.

"It's okay, Abel." Maggie laid a hand on Greene's arm in a gesture of reassurance when the big man stood at the ready. "Blue had engine trouble. When he couldn't get it fixed, he ended up spending the night."

Greene, with that implacable, dark-eyed glare, looked J.D. up and down, taking in his morning stubble, his sleep-mussed hair and his bare body wrapped at the hip with nothing but a blanket and duct tape.

"He got caught in the storm," Maggie added, reacting to Abel's silent appraisal, then turned with a puzzled scowl to J.D. "Your jeans are almost dry," she said, nodding toward the cabin, where she'd hung them by the fire. "I don't hold out much hope for your shoes, though, and your sweatshirt is still in a soaking heap on the dock."

Never taking his eye off Greene, J.D. jerked his head in the general direction of the lake. "I've got a duffel with extra clothes in the plane. With a little luck, there should be something dry in there."

Greene gave J.D.'s bare chest and low-slung blanket another dark once-over. "Might be a good idea if you were to
go get it right now."

Now there was an engraved invitation to leave if he'd ever
heard one. J.D. clenched his jaw, straightened his shoulders and narrowed his eyes at Greene.

"I'll get it," Maggie interjected, her look relaying that
she was both puzzled and annoyed by the presence of
megadoses of testosterone suddenly wafting on the cool
morning air.

"In the meantime," she added, her voice expressing her
irritation, "why don't one of you put on a pot of coffee.
And try to keep it down to glares until I get back, would
you, please? Because, so help me, if I see any bumps or
bruises when I get here, I'm going to add a few more."

With a men-will-be-boys roll of her brown eyes, she left
them to their own devices.

Since it was damned near impossible to look imposing
when your bare skin was crawling with goose pimples and
your nipples were puckered into tight little pebbles in the
nippy morning air, J.D. hiked his blanket higher on his hips
and stalked back into the cabin.

Greene followed a deep breath later, then set about
making a pot of coffee while J.D. poked grumpily around
in the fire.

"You seem to know your way around," J.D. said, irked
beyond measure by that knowledge as Greene pulled the
coffee can out of the first door he opened, in what J.D.
concluded was not a good guess, but the familiarity of a
man who'd done it before.

"And you seem to have imposed—" Greene paused, his
judgmental glare once again skimming the length of J.D.'s
blanket-clad body "—on a friend of mine."

"Friend?" J.D. asked. The one word and the inflection
he gave it clearly told Greene he wanted some clarification
here.

"Friend," Greene echoed after a long moment, but with a clarity of intent and a strength of purpose that satisfied J.D. that friendship was the extent of Greene's involvement with Maggie.

While he was relieved—okay, he was elated—that Greene had no interest in her romantically, J.D. still wasn't comfortable with this man befriending her.

"I was in the mechanic's pool in the Marines," Greene said when the coffee was ready. He poured two cups, then slid one J.D.'s way. "I could take a look at your plane."

"And send me merrily on my way?" J.D. speculated with a sardonic smile, and hoped to hell Greene hadn't already taken a gander under the engine cowling. In the next breath, he figured the big man hadn't looked, because if he'd spotted the pulled fuel line, J.D. might not be standing here in his goose bumps and blankie. Greene would have already had a good start on tearing him apart. At least he'd give it a try, J.D. thought, figuring he could hold his own against him if it came to that.

"Thanks, but no thanks," he said, wrapping his hands around the mug and leaning a hip against the kitchen counter. "I'm sure I can pin down the problem and set her right."

Greene nodded, then turned the tables on J.D. by assuming the role of protector. "How was it that you ended up at Maggie's cabin?"

J.D. fought a grudging respect for the man in that moment. Like it or not, they were, by virtue of his role in the poaching investigation, adversaries. Even knowing that, he had to admire the fact that Greene was looking out for Maggie's best interests. Admiring it, however, was a helluva long way from liking it.

"Maggie and I go way back," he said, offering the same reassurance he'd asked for and received from Greene. "It was my good luck that when I set down yesterday, it was in Blue Heron Bay. My *better* luck that I found Maggie in it."

Put that in your peace pipe and smoke it, J.D. thought,
intending for Greene to accept that J.D.'s involvement with
the lady went far beyond friendship. At least that was the
plan. He wasn't so confident of his plan or his involvement, though, when Maggie swung open the back door and
dumped his duffel on the floor.

"I swear to God, Hazzard, your whole world is held together with duct tape."

J.D. eyed the beat-up duffel, which, he agreed, had a little tape wrapped around it holding it together—all right, a
lot of tape, he conceded upon a closer look.

"The whole world could be held together with that
tape," he said defensively. "It's the best invention since the
propeller."

She just snorted and walked to the cupboard to snag a
mug. "So," she said, filling it with coffee, "you two get
better acquainted?"

"We had a real nice chat," J.D. said with a saccharine-
sweet smile. "And Greene here was just telling me he had
to be on his way, weren't you, Greene?"

The big man ignored him. "Anything you need done
around here, Maggie?"

"Thanks, Abel. But you've taken care of everything. I'm
in good shape."

J.D. perked up at her friendly dismissal, then deflated
like a tire with a fast leak at her next words.

"And just as soon as Hazzard gets on his way, everything will get back to normal."

The look Greene gave J.D. before he drained his mug and
set it on the counter suggested he'd be more than glad to
stick around to make sure that happened.

"I'll slip back around sunset," he said instead, not
needing to add, *and make sure he's gone.*

"No need." Maggie walked him to the door. "I know
you've got things to do. And you don't need to worry about
me. I'm fine."

She seems to be determined to convince everyone she's fine, J.D. concluded with a troubled frown as Hershey bounded back to the cabin and Greene and his wolf dog disappeared into the forest. So far, she was doing a lousy job of it. The only thing she'd convinced him of was that he wasn't comfortable with Maggie setting such stake in Greene's friendship.

J.D. didn't buy into all of the wild stories bandied about the local pubs that embellished and thrived on the legend of Abel Greene. He believed that every man had to choose his own road and his own company, even though Greene did manage to spook the bejesus out of the locals. If Greene, as native to this land as monstrous Norway pines that stood like sentinels along the shore, chose to walk his road alone, far be it from J.D. to cast judgment. Yet he did wonder about him, and though his gut instinct told him Greene was not involved in the black bear poaching, certain facts could not be ignored.

"You've got a lot of nerve, Hazzard."

J.D.'s head came up as Maggie slammed the screen door behind her right after Hershey snuck inside.

"What'd I do?" he asked, as innocent as a babe—he figured he might pull it off since he was at least dressed for the part.

She angled him a dark look. "I don't need you for a keeper *or* a protector."

He didn't bother to deny that that was exactly what he had in mind. "And I suppose you think Greene would fit the bill," he shot back with a nasty glare.

She opened her mouth to say something, closed it, then shook her head. "This is not a conversation I want to have with you. As a matter of fact, I don't want to have *any* conversation with you."

She picked up his duffel and shoved it at him.

He caught it against his middle with a grunt.

"The bedroom is in there."

It was the perfect opening for a little flirtation. "Too bad it isn't the perfect time," J.D. grumbled under his breath as he headed for the bedroom to do the only thing she had in mind.

When he was dressed in dry socks, jeans and a maroon University of Minnesota sweatshirt, he walked back to the kitchen. He figured he was pressing his luck, but he refilled his coffee mug anyway.

Maggie was curled up with her own half-empty mug in an easy chair by the picture window. With the coffeepot in hand, he crossed over to her, then filled the mug she grudgingly extended.

"I hope you know what you're doing," he said carefully.

She let out a tired sigh. "What is that supposed to mean?"

He sat in a chair opposite hers. Wrapping his hands around the warm mug, he looked out over the placid bay.

"It means that you need to be careful about the friends you choose."

She didn't pretend to misunderstand his intent. Her eyes sought his, dark and determined and clouded with fierce, protective anger. "Abel is one of the kindest individuals I know."

J.D. looked away, then enunciated slowly, "I'm just saying you need to be careful."

"No. That's not what you're saying. You aren't saying anything. But you're implying a whole lot. What, exactly, is your problem with Abel?"

He hesitated, then decided she ought to know. "It's not just my problem. It's a problem around the lake. Poaching," he elaborated when her brows furrowed.

She shot him an incredulous look. "Poaching?"

He nodded. "Specifically, black bear."

She blinked, her expression relaying her resistance to the idea. "And you think Abel is responsible?"

"I don't want to think it," he said, realizing as he did that it was true. He didn't want to think the worst of Abel Greene. The tales about Greene's exploits, J.D. dismissed as part fact, part fiction, a by-product of the hermitlike lifestyle the reclusive man had chosen. Greene's unapproachable aloofness and mysterious bearing provided fodder for inventive yarns that relieved the boredom of long winter nights in the Northland. It also made him a target for any kind of speculation.

"I don't want to think it," he repeated for good measure, "but I can't dismiss the fact that Greene has both opportunity and motive."

She stared solemnly into her mug. "Opportunity?"

J.D. leaned forward, knees bent. Propping his forearms on his spread thighs, he dangled his mug between them. "His cabin sits in the middle of some of the most heavily populated colonies of bear in the north woods."

"So does mine," she said heatedly. "That doesn't mean I'm out with a flashlight and a shotgun mowing them down."

"You're forgetting motive."

She inched her knees closer to her chest and rested her chin on them. "By all means, enlighten me about his motive."

"There's a huge profit to be made from the killing of black bears. A segment of Asian culture values their gallbladders for their aphrodisiac powers."

She shuddered in revulsion.

"Yeah," he said, agreeing with her silent commentary. "It's disgusting."

"Abel is not a man who would be motivated by money."

J.D. studied her profile as she stared stubbornly out over the bay. Sunlight shimmered down through the quivering birch and the high bows of the Norway pine, highlighting, defining, playing with the natural beauty of her features, tipping her hair with gold.

"I agree," he said, making himself concentrate on the ugly business at hand. "Revenge, however, can be an even stronger motive."

Her eyes snapped toward his. "Revenge? Are you talking about his scar?"

He shrugged. "The stories are as original as they are varied—ranging from Greene being bushwhacked by a thousand-pound renegade boar, to an attack by a sow protecting her cubs."

"I don't suppose anyone's ever bothered to ask him how it happened."

He gave her a lopsided grin. "I don't suppose anyone's ever had the guts."

That brought a small smile of concession.

"Look, Stretch, I meant it when I said I don't want to believe Greene has anything to do with this, but the fact is, he's on the DNR's list of suspects. That makes him a threat to you in my book."

"Yeah, well, your book has a plot full of holes." She took a long swallow of her coffee. "What have you got to do with all this, anyway?"

"I was patrolling for signs of the poachers when I set down here yesterday."

"Patrolling? What are you, some weekend warrior or something?"

"Not if I can help it. It's just that manpower and machinery are scarce up here. So I volunteer when I can to help out in any number of projects."

"Like?" Her raised brow prompted him.

"Like fire spotting. Sometimes blast patrol south of here on the Iron Range. And sometimes, like now, a little aerial surveillance."

"So you were checking out Abel's place yesterday."

"I was just checking out the area," he clarified. "Abel's place just happens to be in it."

"You'd do well to remember that. Just like *I* happen to be in the middle of it." She gave him a steady look. "Abel isn't responsible for any of that cruel and horrible waste, Blue. He couldn't be."

J.D. let out a deep breath, taken by her loyalty, impressed by her conviction. "I hope you're right. In the meantime, just...just exercise a little judgment where he's concerned, okay?"

She snorted. "This from a man who wouldn't know better judgment if it walked up and announced its presence with a bullhorn."

He let go of a reluctant grin. "You're referring to my plane again, aren't you?"

"I'm referring to your plane."

He smiled confidently. "I'll have to take you up in her someday."

She made a sound of denial. "When the sun sets in the east."

"That sounds like a challenge to me, Ms. Adams."

"Then something's wrong with your hearing too, *Mr.* Hazzard, because what it was was a no, never, not in this lifetime."

He sat back in the chair, taken again by the swift revival of the stubborn, determined Maggie he remembered. "We'll see."

She angled him an exasperated look. "Don't you have some place to be?"

"Other than here, you mean?"

She closed her eyes and counted to ten. "Other than here."

She was weakening. He could see it in her face. It was becoming harder and harder for her to repress a full-fledged grin.

And it was becoming harder and harder for him to dismiss what was happening here as simple flirtation. Ever since he'd spotted her on the dock and his heart had broken into a Minnesota two-step, he'd been in a rare and radical frame of mind. It had taken a dunking in the bay, a night on her sofa and Abel Greene's unexpected appearance to group his thoughts together.

It had taken a deep look inside himself to form a conclusion that now seemed preordained.

"You really don't want me to go, do you, Maggie? It's okay. You can admit it."

She closed her eyes and shook her head. "You know, in my profession I meet a lot of egos. I don't believe, however, that I've encountered one yet that matches yours. You just don't get it. I didn't invite you here. I didn't ask you to stay."

"So what's your point?" he asked with a mock scowl of concentration.

She folded her arms under her breasts and let out a weary breath to keep from smiling. "You're being deliberately obtuse."

"One of my stronger suits."

That little bit of silliness finally earned him a reluctant smile.

"And that's one of yours. You have a beautiful smile, Stretch. You ought to give in to it more often." Just like he decided it was time to give in to his urge to touch her.

His smile faded, however, the moment he touched a finger to the corner of her upturned mouth. His smile faded, his world tilted, then shifted and finally settled him into a truth he could no longer avoid.

"Do you believe in love at first sight, Maggie?" His voice had gone rusty with discovery, soft with certainty and intent.

Her dark gaze skittered to his. He loved the way she was trying her best not to act unnerved by his out-of-the-blue question. He loved the way she shook her head and pretended he wasn't affecting her.

She couldn't quite pull it off, though, J.D. realized with a satisfaction that waylaid her resistance.

"That line didn't work when I was sixteen, Hazzard. Don't count on it working now."

"There are a lot of things I don't count on," J.D. said, inching deeper and deeper into a conviction he'd avoided for the better part of his life. "The weather. The stock market. The Timberwolves making the play-offs." He searched her face, then held her gaze when she made the mistake of meeting his eyes. "But the one thing I *can* count on is how I feel about you."

"Oh, please," she postured with an exaggerated show of impatience but with a wild little spark of hope and panic he found encouraging and heartbreakingly sad.

"Is it really so upsetting Stretch? The prospect that I find you the most fascinating, the most beautiful, the most desirable woman I've ever met?"

She shot off the chair and walked with determined steps toward the kitchen counter. "You need to sort the wheat from the chaff, Hazzard. It's just your hormones talking again. Confusion runs rampant inside that head of yours."

When he walked quietly up behind her, he saw that her hands were shaking as she tried to pour herself more coffee. He reached out a hand. Covered hers. Steadied it. Then he turned her in his arms to face him. She stared hard at a spot in the middle of his chest.

"I think maybe there's a little confusion running amok in someone else's head, too, hmm?" He rubbed her arms in a gesture of comfort when she made herself look at him. "You don't want to react to me, Maggie, but you do. I can see it in your eyes. No. Don't look away."

She drew a brave, thready breath.

"So good at trying to hide your feelings." He squeezed her shoulders lightly. "So bad at pulling it off.

"We'd be good together, Stretch," he murmured, touching a hand to her hair. "Think about it. And while you're at it, think about this."

Lord knows, it was all *he'd* been thinking about. It was also all he could do to keep from devouring her as he lowered his mouth to hers and breathed a feather-light kiss across her lips. When she didn't bolt, he nipped her lightly, feeling her reluctantly melt—and guardedly shift—then lean into him with reckless surrender to match her movements with his. With a groan, he deepened the contact and pulled her closer.

"Think about this," he whispered as he pinned her against the counter with his hips, letting her feel the heat and the length and the strength of his arousal pressed against her belly. "About how much I want you. About how I've always wanted you."

He buried his face in the silk and fragrance of her hair. "And when you're lying alone in your bed tonight wondering what happened this morning, think about the fact that I could be lying there with you. Touching you..." She shivered but didn't pull away when he slid his hand around her ribs and tunneled under her sweatshirt. Her skin was hot to the touch, her breast a sweet, delicate weight that made him shudder then smile when her nipple pebbled beneath the satin of her bra.

"Think of me loving you..."

Pressing his mouth to the irresistible hollow of her throat, he dropped his hand to her waist, then lower, tracing the warm flesh from hip to thigh with his fingers, letting her get used to the idea of intimacy before gently but possessively cupping that heated spot he ached to enter.

Her breath caught in a wispy little shiver.

"Think of me, Stretch," he breathed against her skin, then suppressed a groan when she arched into his hand. "Think of me and know you don't have to be alone."

Six

Maggie watched through the window as Blue taxied out of the bay toward open water. She touched trembling fingers to her mouth, felt the burn of his kiss lingering there, felt the heat of his final caress running like quicksilver through her blood.

"I'll be back," he whispered in that moment before he snagged his duffel, called his dog and walked away.

A devastating combination of desire and despair swamped her as she'd watched him go. She knew he'd keep his promise. He would be back. She was as sure of his return as she was sure that she wanted him gone... if for no other reason than that she needed some breathing room and a chance to get a handle on what was happening to her.

It's just sexual, she told herself staunchly. He was a beautiful man. But she was used to beautiful men. Just because this man had an unprecedented ability to flip response switches she hadn't known she had, didn't mean there was anything other than sex propelling his actions.

She sighed deeply, damned herself for a fool and pressed her forehead against the windowpane. Sex was not salvation. Sex was slavery. Sex was controlling and manipulative and disabling and never again would she mistake it for love.

Never again would she let it be enough.

She would not let herself get involved in a physical relationship with Blue. At least the logical side of her brain told her she wouldn't. Just like the logical side of her brain kept reminding her that less than twenty-four hours had passed since he'd dropped out of the sky and back into her life. Given those circumstances, any sane woman wouldn't be thinking about sex or salvation or anything in between.

Logic, however, had little to offset the aching loneliness that enveloped her as she stood there watching the sunlight glint off the nose of the Cessna as it gained speed then took flight.

Fool, fool, fool, she berated herself mentally. As inconceivable as it seemed, she'd let Blue get to her. He made her want to believe what he felt for her was more than physical, made her wish for something that couldn't be. His incorrigible smile, his teasing wit, his total lack of pretense had all teamed forces against her resolve and weakened her resistance. She wanted—for the first time since the last of her innocence had been stolen—to believe in love. And she wanted to believe Blue could give it to her.

More than disgusted with herself, she turned away from the window, determined to shake it off. Determined to ignore the overwhelming sense of loss that clutched at her heart and twisted. Feeling very tired suddenly and grappling with a frustration that was rivaled only by confusion, she stripped off her sweats and headed for the shower.

"It's time to regroup," she lectured herself. "You came here to be alone. To forget. And to heal."

Until Blue had arrived so unexpectedly she'd come a long way in accomplishing her goals. Now that she was alone again, she could get on with the business at hand.

After drying her hair, she slipped on a lightweight cotton knit sweater and chinos, refilled her coffee cup and walked down to the dock. A flotilla of pelicans glided like a great white fleet near the distant shore. Overhead, the sun burned bright on the crystal-bright surface of the bay. The clear glacial water mirrored the cotton white clouds drifting like dollops of whipped cream against the cerulean blue backdrop of a pure and endless sky.

It was so beautiful here. So blessedly, yet so unyieldingly remote. She sipped her coffee, hoping that in addition to being isolated, it was far enough away from New York to keep Rolfe at bay. Paris hadn't been. The first time she'd decided to make the break from him, even an ocean between them hadn't been enough.

She breathed deep of the storm-cleansed morning air, savoring the sunlight, embracing the silence. She wasn't fooling herself. She knew that if she were ever to get on with her life, she would have to confront Rolfe. The prospect clenched her insides into alternating knots of nausea and dread. She would confront him. But she needed more time. More time to become strong enough to face him down, to stick to her convictions, to not be swayed by his pleading and his threats and his demand for gratitude.

She'd felt a tentative growth in her strength of will until yesterday. Until Blue Hazzard had buzzed into her bay, rocked the rock she was standing on and sent her into this lapse of resolution. She still couldn't believe his nerve. The man had just burst into her life after all these years, had the gall to kiss her—repeatedly—and ask her if she believed in love at first sight.

She should be irritated as hell, not only with his insufferable persistence but with his interference in her life. Yet every time she thought of him, she got this warm, fuzzy feeling that made her think of safety, sweet seduction and sizzling sex. She fought a slow, reluctant smile as she pictured him again in her pink bathrobe.

Unsuccessful at willing the memory away, she let out a deep sigh. The man was trouble.

The man was also good to his word. She'd known he would be. Late the next afternoon, he was back. And she still didn't know what she was going to do about him.

J.D. knew exactly what he was going to do about Maggie.

He was going to make her smile and make her laugh. Then he was going to make her his. Once he'd accomplished that, he was going to find out her most guarded secret. The one that put that cornered, harried look in her eyes and made his heart ache with both anger and despair. When he discovered what it was, he was going to fix it.

"Would you listen to yourself, Hazzard?" he mumbled aloud as he taxied the Cessna into the bay and beached her on the sand. "You've developed a real Lancelot complex here."

He'd never been anyone's white knight. He'd never wanted to be. He wanted to be Maggie's.

"You also sound like some love-struck puppy. No offense, Hersh," he added as Hershey rolled soulful brown eyes his way from the shotgun seat.

"You're even talking to yourself. Love-struck it is," he conceded, unable to muster up the will to be disgusted with himself as he shouldered open the cockpit door and climbed outside as eager as a kid on his first date.

He'd had two days and two nights to think about his reactions to Maggie. Two days and two nights out of 365 days of each of the last fifteen years didn't seem like much time in the overall scheme of things. And while his practical side warned him he was being far too hasty, his gut reaction was to go for broke.

Bottom line, he'd fallen for her the first time he'd set eyes on her all those years ago. He'd been drifting in a foggy sort of limbo ever since, not even realizing she was the woman who had put his life on hold in the relationship department.

"Full speed ahead," he said with a grin as he scaled the rock slope, hiked through the woods and broke into her front yard.

She was waiting for him on the deck. Her look was guarded. Her lips were set in a hard, tight line. Yet her eyes, those glorious pepper-brown eyes, were lit with the softest glow, the prettiest spark as he walked toward her.

He was seventeen all over again. He was Mickey Rooney meeting Judy Garland just before the finale that called for a huge, juicy kiss. His heart hammered, his palms sweat and his friend, Mr. Libido, was determined to embarrass him with a total lack of tact and inconceivably bad timing.

He stopped and planted one foot on the bottom deck step. Leaning forward with his elbow propped on his knee, he worked on regaining control and hiding his physical reaction.

He smiled innocently up at her. "Hey, Stretch. How's it going?"

True to form, she crossed her arms snugly beneath her breasts. Also true to form, she had big plans on being resistant as hell.

It was enough to settle him down. "That glad to see me, huh?"

She just blinked hard and looked out over the bay. He braved the steps to stand beside her.

"I brought you something."

When her gaze flashed to his, he extended the package he'd kept out of sight behind his back.

With reluctant curiosity, she took it, opened it, then frowned. "Fish?"

"Not only is she pretty, she's astute. I love that in a woman."

Again, she looked down at the package of walleye fillets, then back at him. "You brought me fish." It was more of a bewildered statement than a question.

He gave her his most guileless grin. "Sorry. I couldn't find any flowers."

A soft smile snuck up on her before she could squelch it. "What else would I expect from a man who thinks duct tape is an alloy."

"Ah, humor. I like that in a woman, too." He liked even better the implication that she was expecting something. That was good. It meant she hadn't altogether dismissed the idea of him coming back.

"I figure if we were a little closer to civilization, I'd be taking you out to some glitzy restaurant about now. Since that can't happen, I decided the next best thing was to bring dinner to you."

"I don't recall being asked if I would want to go out to dinner with you."

She looked so cute sitting there, her back stiff, working so hard on being huffy. "Well, that's a given," he said, playing for another smile and almost winning one. "But, I made room for the possibility that if, by some stretch of the imagination, you were resistant to the idea, you'd at least have the sense not to turn down a free meal."

She held her ground. "I don't suppose it would matter if I said I wasn't hungry."

"Actually, that should work out just fine. I'm always hungry."

She narrowed her eyes. "And if I said I don't cook?"

He grinned hugely. "I'd say I never expected you to. Besides, when it comes to frying fish, nobody does it better than me."

She let out a long-suffering sigh. "You have an uncanny way of habitually reaffirming a conclusion I've drawn about you."

"That I'm irresistible?" he suggested brightly.

"That you could never be mistaken for being ego-impaired. Without exception, you are the most arrogant man I've ever met."

"Arrogant?" He tried hard to look wounded. "That's a little harsh, don't you think? Aggressive, maybe."

She sniffed. "Try obnoxious."

"Persistent fits better, I think."

"Badgering fits perfectly."

He was enjoying this, and if she'd just loosen up and let herself admit it, he suspected she was enjoying it too. He winked at her and tried again. "Persuasive?"

This time her mouth quirked. "Belligerent."

"Determined," he countered, sensing her weakening. "I'm a determined man, Maggie mine."

She bristled right up again. "I am *not* your Maggie."

He'd gone a little too far with that one but decided to go for broke anyway. "Not yet, you're not. But you will be," he promised with a meaningful look. "Just as soon as you say the word."

That shut her up. It made him grin—something he seemed to continually feel the need to do since he'd found her again. Just like she obviously felt the need to back away from this conversation. That cornered look had crept over her face again.

"So you don't cook," he said, changing tacks and giving her that out. "Not a problem. Watch and learn."

He snagged the fish from her hands, sauntered on by her and walked into the cabin.

"By all means, make yourself at home."

Ignoring her sarcasm, he let the screen door bump shut behind him and assured her over his shoulder, "Oh, I plan to."

Her mumbled, "Now why does that not surprise me," didn't even slow his steps as he headed for the kitchen and started rummaging around in her cabinets for a frying pan.

In the end, he'd had to play on her basic generosity to trick her into helping him with the meal. She contributed by making a salad while he fried the fish in a light coating of corn meal and cooked potatoes and carrots and onions in a separate pan.

By the time she'd set the table and they'd had several wonderfully accidental run-ins near the sink and stove in the cramped area, the delicious cooking aromas and his constant banter had begun to loosen her up a little. Her responses to his running commentary on everything from the weather to colorful stories about the locals and his business adventures had stretched out from stilted "uh-huhs" to the occasional "you're making that up" or "you are so full of it, Hazzard." She'd even smiled a couple of times without first thinking if she should let herself. He began to take heart.

"So, what do you think?" he asked anxiously as she sat with her fork poised over her plate after swallowing a delicate mouthful of fish.

"I think—" she paused to sigh with obvious pleasure "—that you could have a position as a chef at any number of haute cuisine establishments on the Left Bank."

He gave her a huge, proud smile. "That good, huh?"

She nodded. "That good. Too good, in fact. It'll take me a week to work off what I'm planning to eat tonight."

"Oh, I don't know. From where I sit, it appears you could handle a few more pounds without ruining those fine lines."

"Well," she said, getting adept at deflecting his teasing innuendos, "it may not make any difference, anyway. Since I've been out of circulation so long, and since I walked away from several contracts already in the works, I may not be in demand when I'm ready to work again. *If* I decide to work again," she added with a thoughtful look across the table and out the window.

J.D. wanted to zero in on her cryptic statement. He made himself hold back, purposely keeping the banter light. "From what I've seen of your career, it occurs to me that if you didn't want to, you probably wouldn't have to work again."

She nodded. "Not for financial reasons, that's true. Retirement at my age seems a bit premature, though, don't you think?"

"No challenge in that," he agreed. "So, if you decide not to go back to modeling, what would you like to do?"

When she spoke, it was apparent that she had given the subject some serious thought. "I might try my hand on the other side of the camera."

He propped his forearm on the table and leaned back in the chair, considering. "Really? Well, they say that within every actor is a director waiting to burst out. Maybe the same holds true for models."

She shrugged. "Maybe."

She became unnaturally silent then and stayed that way throughout the remainder of the meal, no matter how hard he played for a reaction.

When it was over, he insisted: he washed, she dried. And in the homey intimacy of shared soap suds and softening daylight, he felt a slow and gentle relaxing of her guard again.

One step at a time, Hazzard, he cautioned himself later as he held himself in check with a painfully brief goodbye kiss on her cheek, collected Hershey and flew off into the sunset.

He had a plan, he kept assuring himself. And as soon as he figured out what it was, he was going to put it into action.

* * *

As it turned out, the plan developed kind of naturally. He kept showing up. She kept letting him. How could he not just fly with it?

Not a day went by during the next two weeks that he didn't "drop in" to bring her more fish, or to see how she was doing, or to try to make her laugh or roll those pretty eyes of hers or to simply look at him as if she was trying to figure out how far she could let herself trust him.

He didn't ply her for more information. He didn't press for more intimacy. He talked and he laughed and he gave her time and room and his company. And he steered clear of any conversation about the poachers, and his niggling concern that her friend Abel Greene might still be involved.

Instead, he concentrated on her. He let her get to know him, get to like him, and more importantly, get used to having him around. They went on long walks together; sometimes they even ran together. He fixed a leaky water pipe with his duct tape, they gave a disgruntled Hershey a bath in the lake and one afternoon he actually brought her flowers instead of fish, then helped her plant them in the flower bed in the front yard.

Tonight, two weeks after he'd discovered her in the bay, he decided his slow and easy approach had been a wise choice of tactics. They sat side by side near the fire he'd made in the stone ring that he'd built for her by the shore. Hershey chased fireflies and made her grin as the moon rose high and full, reflecting its light like a shimmering yellow ribbon on the surface of the bay. It came to him as they shared the special night, that this was the first day she hadn't reminded him it was getting late and suggested it was past time he headed for base.

He took great stock in that omission. Even greater in the soft looks and considering glances she kept casting his way when she thought he wasn't looking. Hope rode high and strong inside him as he let the land and the water and the night infuse the moment with the magic that had brought him back year after year and had led him straight to her.

The lake spoke its own special language at night. The sipping sounds of water lapped in an endless, gentle caress to mate with the welcome embrace of the shore. The occasional muted echo of a distant voice carried across the bay from a far-off cabin or campsite. Fallen leaves and dried pine needles rustled in the undergrowth as timid night creatures scurried across the forest floor. All were sounds inherent to the north, yet as elusive as the lake breeze that whispered around and between them, drawing them to a rich, new awareness of each other. The sensation was as unifying as it was unique. As was the color of the night.

But for the starlight and moon glow, the night was filled with infinite shades of black, from the inky ripples on the water, to the jagged tree line etched along a cloudless horizon, to the shadows dancing on the shore. Even Maggie, her famous profile silhouetted against those definitive, deep hues, was a part of it. Never more than this night, he sensed her affinity with the quiet, peaceful perfection, uncluttered by population and city noise, uncomplicated by pressure and pretense.

He also sensed her mood change as he watched her. Sensed a gradual lifting of her guard, a mellow yielding of her defenses.

"Are you for real, Hazzard?"

Her question filtered out of the darkness, soft, without preamble, starkly open and full of hope. She faced the fire and the lake, never looking his way, never giving any indication that he was even on her mind.

He didn't pretend to misunderstand. She was asking for something to believe in. She was asking him not to hurt her if she gave in to the needs she'd been denying and to the desire she'd been so determined to fight.

His answer was sure and uncategorical. "As real as it gets, Stretch."

She let out a deep breath before turning to him, her eyes searching his in the moonlight. Searching, seeking, yearning to believe in the truth of his answer.

"I don't know what—or who—happened to you to make it so hard for you to trust me," he said carefully. "Maybe someday you'll feel you can tell me."

Her eyes hardened, then focused on some very real and well-remembered pain before she looked away.

"I don't know what happened," he repeated, "and right now, I don't care," he continued, wanting to assure her he was no threat to her privacy. "I only know I care about you.

"I want to be with you, Maggie." He rose from his chair to stand in front of her. "I want to talk with you and laugh with you. But more than breathing, right now, I want to make love with you."

She closed her eyes.

The silence thickened. The distance that he'd thought had finally been breached stretched into infinity as he watched her face and prayed he hadn't blown it.

"You missed your cue, Stretch," he said gently as he knelt in front of her and took her hands in his. "This is the part where you're supposed to say, I want to make love with you, too."

He tried to keep it playful. Tried to make light of something that had become more important to him than life. But even he wasn't a total master of his emotions and he knew that when she met his gaze she understood he was nervous about this step, too. While his heart had never taken the beating that hers must have, he was making it vulnerable right now, giving her the power to bruise and bloody it.

Her voice was full of hesitation and regret when she finally spoke. "I need to be up-front with you, Hazzard. I don't have anything to give to a long-term relationship."

Her straightforward conviction made his heart clench. As admissions went, it was a whopper, both discouraging and enlightening. Discouraging because he knew she believed what she said. Enlightening because it revealed that she wanted to give and that she wanted to give to him.

He touched a hand to her hair where the moon reflected off the water, dancing along the fine strands, making it shimmer like raw silk.

"So what do you say we don't look that far ahead? What do you say we take this in baby steps, one at a time? We could both be in for a nice surprise at the end of the journey."

She swallowed hard. "Or a huge disappointment."

"Possibly," he agreed, squeezing her hands lightly then running his thumbs in a soothing caress along the backs of them. "Or it could be the best thing that's ever happened to either one of us.

"There's one thing about it, though," he added when her hesitance told him she needed one final push. "We'll never know if we don't give it a try."

"And what if it doesn't work? What happens then?"

She tried to mask the urgency of her question. She didn't pull it off, leaving him wondering why the beginning of their relationship seemed to hinge on what happened if it ended. It was not what he considered an auspicious note to start out on. But, as she searched his face, commanding him to give her question import, he realized how critical it was to her.

"What happens then," he said levelly, and prayed they'd never have to deal with that particular dilemma, "is that we say nice try, admit it wasn't to be and part as friends."

The relief that washed across her face told him it was exactly what she needed to hear. The promise she extracted from him then made him all the more determined to find out why.

"Promise me," she said, gripping his hands tightly in hers. "Promise me exactly that. When it's over, we simply part. No expectations. No regrets. No postmortem."

"*If* it's ever over," he said, correcting her but addressing her with the sincerity her intensity demanded. "I promise. The break will be clean."

While he wasn't particularly pleased by the entire turn of their conversation, he was relieved when the tension lines around her mouth eased and were replaced by a small, tentative smile.

He returned that smile, watching her eyes glitter like starlight, more determined than ever to make his promise moot. He wasn't going to give her any reason to want to end it. He was going to give her a thousand reasons to go the distance.

"Are we square now, Maggie?" he asked softly.

She looked away, looked back at him, then nodded.

"Good." He gave her hands a light squeeze. "Now... does this mean I finally get to see you naked?"

His outrageous question brought a light to her eyes. It was a light he'd caught fleeting glimpses of over the past couple of weeks but one she'd always fought giving in to. She didn't fight it now. She shook her head and smiled with him the way he'd meant for her to.

"Has anyone ever suggested that finesse may not be one of your strong points?"

"Never," he said, deadpan. "But, if that particular approach didn't spin your propeller, I've got another one."

"I can hardly wait."

With their hands still locked together, he drew her to her feet. The moon held silent counsel, the water song urged him on as he wrapped her in his arms.

"Come with me, Maggie." He pressed his lips to her hair. "Come with me to the cabin. Let me take you to your bed."

He felt her heartbeat dance against his chest, rivaling the rhythm of his own as his hands glided down the exquisite slope of her back. Felt her shiver with wanting and go boneless with desire as he cupped and enticed her hips into more intimate contact with his.

"Let me undress you, and touch you...with my mouth...with my hands." He bent his head to her neck, whispering his wants, relaying his need as he tracked a string of soft, biting kisses along her skin. "Let me love you, Maggie...I promise, I'll go as slow as you want...take as long as you need."

He raised his head, meeting the shimmering passion that glimmered in her eyes. "And when it's over," he murmured, brushing his mouth to hers, "let me start all over again."

Maggie searched the face of this man who had rekindled twin fires of hope and longing to burn warm and low inside her. She searched his eyes and saw straight through to his heart. What she saw there made the cynic inside her give way to the yearnings she fought every day to deny. Even though she knew she was making a mistake, even though she knew his good intentions might turn to bad in the stark, harsh light of day, she let the need to believe take over. Even if it was only for tonight.

He'd been so gentle the past two weeks. So patiently attentive, so sensitively and silently persuasive. She'd run out of arguments a week ago. She'd run out of conviction before then. He was too much to resist, offered so much more than she dared hope for. But hope won out as he held her in the moonlight and, with the promise of his words and the caress of his eyes, touched her heart in ways it had never been touched before.

It wasn't wise to let it happen. And it wasn't too late to stop this, she reminded herself in a last-ditch effort to court her fears. If she got a handle on things right now, she could still convince him it wasn't what she wanted. She could convince him, but she couldn't lie to herself. She liked how he made her feel. She liked the fact that he didn't make any bones about his attraction to her. She'd had enough game-playing in her life. More than enough coy innuendos and power-motivated attention. An excess of walking a tight-rope of uncertainty that had been orchestrated to diminish her sense of self-worth.

None of that would be a factor in a relationship with Blue Hazzard. A relationship with Blue would be both playful and provocative, sexy and sweet, sumptuous and soul-ful—just like the man. But while all those descriptions fit him, she also sensed an inherent goodness in him that would prohibit him from ever using any of those ploys against her. That was the ultimate promise she would not break. She would not be used again.

"I want to trust you," she whispered, not realizing she'd spoken out loud until he drew her roughly and urgently against him.

"Then do." His ardent words enveloped her, coarse and commanding, committed to persuade, determined to en-tice. "Look at me and know that you can."

She did as he asked. She looked at him. Only him, blocking out the memory of another man's self-serving promises and empty words. For too long, she hadn't been strong enough to overcome Rolfe's dominance. She'd let him use her and abuse her—all in the name of love. All for his love of power and *her* money.

Power and money would not be a motivating factor for Blue. The only power he believed in was the power of love and his ability to sustain it.

Blue was nothing like Rolfe. His motives, like the sym-metry of his strong angular features, were as honest as his beauty. The desire burning in his eyes was for her as a woman, not as a commodity.

"I believe you," she murmured, no longer caring that she might be chasing a pipe dream.

Letting the moment convince her she was strong enough to survive a relationship, she leaned into his heat and his hardness, giving herself over to his keeping in a major leap of faith. "At this moment, there's nothing I believe more."

Seven

Shadows played along the knotty-pine-paneled walls of the bedroom. Moon glow and the lake breeze infused the room with soft shadings, the scent of the forest and the warmth of the Minnesota night.

"You're shivering," he whispered as he led her to the bed. "Do you want me to close the window?"

Her eyes caught the moonlight like glittering stars as she chafed her hands along her arms and shook her head. "I'm not cold."

He touched a hand to her hair. "Nervous then?"

She lowered her head.

"Hey." Curling a finger under her chin, he tipped her head up. "Don't think you're the only one with a case of the jitters."

She smiled ruefully. "You expect me to believe that?"

His hands went to her waist and rested lightly there. "I've been talking pretty big, Stretch. And don't forget who you are. If you think for one minute that I'm not worried about disappointing you, you have no idea of the power you wield.''

Her eyes grew brittle with anger, then frosted over with a disappointment that was no less baffling. She turned away from him and stared out the window.

He stood there, head cocked in confusion, and took stock of their conversation. "What? What did I say?"

"This is about power?" she demanded, as if she already knew the answer and it sickened her. "This is about who I am?"

The tremor in her voice gave him pause, then relayed with aching clarity the source of her agitation. He should have known. He should have realized she'd spent the past several years guarding her feelings and protecting her affections against the predators and pretenders who prowled the world she lived in.

Walking up behind her, he cupped her shoulders in his hands. "It's been pretty rough, huh?" he asked gently. "Everybody wants a piece of the superstar? Everybody wants something for nothing? Everybody wants to win your favor to add to their own importance."

The stiffening of her slight frame beneath his hands confirmed his suspicions. He turned her in his arms to face him.

"There's something you've lost sight of here, Stretch. There's no one here but you and me. And there's no one here who wants anything from you but who you are.

"Yes," he continued when her eyes flashed fire. "*Who you are*. Maggie Adams, the same woman with the same qualities that have made you special to me since you were sixteen years old. I felt your power over me way back then. I still do.

"But what you're forgetting, Stretch, is that I wanted you before the world ever knew your face or your name. I *still* want you," he whispered, and knew his voice was less than steady. "I'd want you if you pumped gas. I want you in spite of the fact that if I let it, your fame could intimidate me long before it would entice me."

Cupping her cheeks in his palms, he tipped her face to his, his voice dropping to a ragged whisper. "I want you as a woman—just a woman. I always have and, God help me, I think I always will. And damn right I'm scared—right down to my toes—that I'll let you down after finally convincing you I'm worth the effort."

Her eyes glittered with aching measures of relief and guilt as they searched his. "I'm sorry," she whispered, touching her fingers to his jaw.

He turned his mouth into her palm and pressed a kiss there. "No need."

"Big need," she insisted. "I wasn't being fair. You're nothing like him. Even if you tried, you never could be."

J.D. didn't know who the "him" was that she referred to. He wasn't even sure she was aware she'd spoken aloud. And while the thought of someone treating her as anything less than special knotted his gut with rage, right now he didn't want to know. He didn't want to think about any other man in her life. He didn't want Maggie to think about him, either.

He wrapped her protectively in his arms, hugging her fiercely, loving the way she nestled trustingly against him, reigniting the desire that had brought them both this far.

He pressed a kiss to the top of her head, then laid his cheek against her hair. "This is nice," he whispered, his bid for control making his voice gritty.

"Umm," she agreed with a soft, indulgent sigh. "I can think of something nicer."

If his heart beat any harder, he was afraid he'd bruise her. "Nicer?" he managed in a sandpapery rasp.

She tipped her head back, her eyes meeting his with a bold, enticing sparkle. "Let's see some skin, Hazzard. Lord knows, you've taken every other opportunity you could to show it to me."

A crooked smile tilted one corner of his mouth. "Anything to please the lady."

His hands were shaking as he backed away far enough to peel his shirt over his head and toss it toward the corner of the room. A ragged, shuddering breath escaped him as her heavy-lidded gaze connected with his, then slid slowly to his chest. Her hands were quick to follow.

Her fingers were long and elegant, and paganly erotic as she skimmed them over the burning flesh of his chest. Exploring, enticing, driving him wild then taking him to the edge of control when she moved to the snap on his jeans and popped it open.

"Oh, damn," he muttered on a groan and stilled her questing hands. "You . . . we . . . I . . ."

"Need to slow down?" she suggested huskily as he realized he was gripping her hands so tightly he'd made her wince.

"Yes," he groaned, and dragged in a serrated breath.

With a self-deprecating smile, he released her. "We *definitely* need to slow down or one of us is going to be finished before the other one even gets started."

"I wouldn't mind," she offered softly.

Her unselfish offer unhinged him. And with those selfless, guileless words, J. D. Hazzard fell completely in love. Over the cliff, off the charts, to the core of the universe, in love. Oh, he'd known that was where this was heading. He'd just never realized how irrevocably committed he was to her until this moment when she, without hesitation, put his pleasure before her own.

"*I'd* mind," he insisted, regaining his control with a determination that overrode his aching need for release. "I would mind very much. If my mother taught me anything, it was to err in the favor of courtesy. Ladies first, Stretch. At least it will be if you could find it in you to join me in that bed."

"Somehow," she said, her smile feminine and confident as she reached for the top button of her blouse and slipped it free, "I don't think your mother had lovemaking in mind when she taught you that lesson."

A shudder eddied through him. "And somehow I really regret bringing my mother into this conversation. As a matter of fact..." His hands dropped to help her with the remaining buttons, then peeled the blouse from her shoulders. "I don't think conversation lends itself in any way to this moment."

"No?"

"No," he whispered, then stopped breathing when she reached behind her back, unfastened her bra and let it drift to the floor at her feet.

"Maggie..."

Nothing was more yielding than the sweet, lush haven of her body. Nothing was more giving or more inviting than when she finally lay naked beside him and her long, golden length was stretched out across the moon-kissed sheets of the bed.

Nothing was more sacred than her unqualified trust when he assured her, "You're safe with me. I'd never do anything to hurt you, Maggie. I'd never put you at risk... and I've taken care that I'd never be at risk either."

"In all the ways that count, I do feel safe with you, Blue...just as you can feel safe with me."

J.D. leaned over her, bracing his forearms on either side of her ribs. "This is how I've imagined you," he murmured, cupping one ivory breast in his hand, then lifting as he lowered his mouth to taste her. "For so long now."

She made a soft, pleasured sound when he nuzzled his lips against a sweetly peaked nipple in acquaintance. She threaded her fingers through his hair, then sucked in her breath in an erotic little gasp when acquaintance transcended to a slow, thorough exploration with his tongue and lips and teeth. And when he'd explored to his satisfaction and drew her deeply into his mouth to possess her as his body demanded, she arched, her abdominal muscles contracting, her heart dancing beneath the heel of his hand where it rested against her ribs.

"Hazzard." She sighed and rolled into him, tangling those glorious silken legs with his and urging him closer.

He raised his head and met dark eyes glistening with desire, shimmering with need. Imploring, impatient, the look she gave him teamed with her body's restless rhythm, urging him to complete the act he'd started.

"We've got all night, Maggie. There's no rush." To prove it, he brushed his thumb slowly across her parted lips. She caught the fleshy pad of the tip between her teeth, nipping him lightly before enticing it inside her mouth, where her tongue stroked with a rhythm that matched the one her hips had set against his.

"Then again," he ground out as she rolled to her back, urging him to cover her body with his, and made a place for him between her thighs. "I could be wrong."

He dropped his head to the silken hollow beneath her jaw and clenched every muscle in his body when she rocked her hips against him. "Have mercy, Maggie. I wanted to make this slow for you."

"Make it slow later," she whispered urgently, and reached between them to find him, clasp him in her hot, elegant hands and guide him to her welcoming heat. "Right now...just make it happen."

He was more than willing to oblige her. Not so willing to drag himself out of the sensual fog enveloping him and take care of the business of protecting her. Not willing—there was nothing he wanted more than to have nothing between them—but bound by responsibility to do it anyway.

Separating himself from the delicious contact of her body, however, was not an option. He banded an arm around her waist and dragged her with him to the edge of the bed. With haste and decided lack of patience, he reached down and groped around on the floor, found his jeans and wrestled a packet of protection from the pocket. He was shaking so badly from the effort to maintain control that she smiled crookedly and took it from his fumbling fingers.

"You'll pay for this," he promised as he tugged her back to the center of the bed. He groaned as with an agonizingly evocative touch, she rolled the condom into place. "You'll pay dearly."

"I seem to recall hearing that threat from you before."

His breath stalled when she nudged her cleft against the tip of his straining arousal. "When I get done making a panting fool of myself over you," he gritted out, "I'm going to make so good on that threat you'll be begging for...mercy."

Lacing her fingers behind his neck, she brought his mouth down to hers and whispered against his lips. "Anything you say, Hazzard. Only, please...say it later."

He couldn't have said anything at that point if his life had hung in the balance. She'd drained him not only of the power of speech but of every cognizant thought in his head but one: making her his.

He took her mouth with a deep, probing kiss, his tongue delving in and out in a sweet, enticing prelude to his body's slow penetration of hers.

Making a cave of his arms around her head, he knotted his hands in her hair and tried to hold himself together as he sank deep. She was wet heat and sweet salvation as her body stretched to accommodate him, then clenched to welcome him home.

Until that point—when she clutched and caressed and called his name in a breathless cry of exultation and greed— he'd clung foolishly to the conviction that he still had a fighting chance of pulling out of this tailspin of mind-numbing, pleasure-induced oblivion to tend to her needs.

In truth, he'd never had a prayer. The moment she slid those long, supple legs along his, wrapped them around his hips and locked him against her, he surrendered completely to the pleasure of her body, to the wonder that was her own drugging passion.

He wanted to bury himself so deeply inside her he'd never find his way out. Yet the wild, delicious friction of sliding into her lush heat compelled him to withdraw slowly, relishing the burn, anticipating the molten sensation of his return.

Watching her face, feeding his flames, he plunged back into her with a series of hard, swift strokes that careened him straight over the edge of control. His breath hissed out of his body in a tortured groan when he ignited, then burst into a brilliant arch of white-hot flame. Burying deep, crushing her to him to extend the contact and the force of his devastating climax, he rode with the most excruciating pleasure he'd ever known. And in the moment when he exploded inside her, he died . . . an exquisite, glorious death, happily drawing his last breath before being born again to draw his first in the wonder of this woman's arms.

Maggie ran her hands in a lazy, contented glide along the damp planes of Blue's muscled back. His weight was glorious and heavy above her, his breathing labored, his heart pounding like thunder against her breast.

"For the record, Stretch . . ." His ragged breath fanned her cheek before he nuzzled, with tender exhaustion, beneath her jaw. "Even though it was your fault, that's the first and the last promise I'll ever break to you."

She pressed a soft smile against his throat. "Do you hear me complaining?"

With great effort, he managed to brace himself on his elbows above her. His tousled blond hair, mussed beautifully by her hands moments earlier, fell across blue eyes still clouded with latent passion and raw regret.

"But I promised you so much more."

She raised a hand to brush the hair from his eyes. "Like you said, we've got all night."

With a contented groan, he rolled to his back, taking her with him, reversing their positions. As she looked down at his beautiful face, his gaze searched hers with a look of telltale guilt that made her heart swell.

"You all right?"

She blinked slowly. "I'm fine. In fact, I'm terrific. And you..." She sucked in her breath, stunned when she felt the sure, swelling length of his arousal growing against her belly. "You have amazing recuperative powers."

His smile was slow, sly and seductive. "I told you I was going to make it up to you. Consider this the first install-ment in an effort to make it worth your wait."

Her body's reaction to his velvety promise was instant and electric. Heat infiltrated the night and her blood with a quick, aching anticipation. Sensation tingled along her skin, making her aware of the cool drift of the night breeze through the window, the warm, musky scent of sex cling-ing to the sheets and her skin, the hot, hard body of the beautiful man beneath her.

She bit her lower lip to keep from crying out when his huge, caressing hands slid down the length of her back, cupping and kneading her buttocks before drifting lower. Watching her face, reading her need, he gripped her thighs in a gentle hold and urged her to part them.

"Open up, Maggie. Let me show you how special you are to me."

She swallowed hard and gave herself over to him, spreading her legs until she straddled his hips, her knees digging into the mattress at his sides.

His fingers spread wide along her thighs as his hands traveled to her hips and urged her to sit up, astride him. "Let me see how beautiful you are."

With a slumberous stretch, she obeyed again, the drowsy, sexy look in his eyes convincing her his requests were motivated not by his need to control but by tenderness and a longing to please her.

She felt open and exposed yet as wanton as a woman in love when he lay silent beneath her, his gaze and his hands devouring her body in the soft night shadows.

"So beautiful. So special, Maggie mine," he murmured as he raised his hands to the wild tangle of her hair and with widespread fingers raked it away from her face. "Tell me how to touch you. Tell me what you like."

"Anything." The huskiness of her admission told them both the power he held over her. His eyes flared with the fire of desire. "Anything you want to do," she confessed shamelessly as she closed her eyes and rocked against his hips. With her back arched, her hair trailing down her back, she showed him with her motions, urged him with her sighs, that all she needed was him beneath her, him inside her to make her come alive.

A groan of passion too powerful to suppress ripped from his throat as he reared up and, with the grip of his strong hands circumferencing her ribs, lowered his head to her offered breast. He consumed her with rough, open-mouth kisses, suckled her with a hunger born of her compliance, then pleasured her with a selflessness inspired by her giving.

He drew her deeply into his mouth then pulled away, teasing, tempting, tormenting her to a restless yearning that had her crying his name.

"Are you wet for me, Maggie?" he demanded, raking his teeth across her nipple as he reached between their bodies and sought his answer.

He groaned his pleasure against her distended nipple. "Sweet, sweet woman," he growled as he eased a finger inside her slick heat and finessed her to yet another plane of need.

She moved against his questing caress, moaned when he found the swollen, sensitive nub of her femininity with his thumb and gave in to his velvet whisper. "Come for me...come for me."

Pleasure coiled, swelled and exploded inside her with a wrenching series of powerful, shimmering detonations that stole her breath, robbed her strength and left her limp and spent against him.

He wrapped her in his arms, cradled her face against his chest and rocked her until her trembling subsided. When she could find the strength, she dragged her hair from her eyes, then looped her arms around his neck, cuddling closer. "You...you sure know how to make good on a promise," she managed on a breathless sigh of contentment.

He chuckled and, gathering her tighter against him, shifted, lifted, then settled her on her back beneath him. "Promises," he corrected as his mouth tracked in a maddeningly slow path down the length of her body. "Multiple promises," he murmured as he gently bit her hip point, then moved to the inside of her thigh before cupping her hips in his hands and tilting her to his mouth. "Multiple pleasures for my lady."

With exquisite attention to her needs, he proceeded to fulfill those promises...as she proceeded to come apart for him again in what proved to be a night of untold pleasures.

"Are you asleep?"

Blue's voice drifted into her slumber on a hazy cloud of contentment and exhaustion.

She burrowed her face deeper into the pillow, then sighed with pleasure when she felt his hand stroke slowly up and down the length of her bare back. If she'd been a cat, she'd have purred when his mouth followed everywhere his hand had been.

"Wake up, Stretch, I want to show you something."

She cracked an eye open, realized it was the middle of the night and tried to pull the sheet over her head. "Whatever it is, can't it wait until morning?"

"Not this time. Come on. You'll be sorry if you miss it."

With a resigned groan, she rolled to her back so she could look at him. If he hadn't reached out and grabbed her, she'd have spilled right off the side of the bed.

"Has anyone ever suggested that you take up an enormous amount of sheet space?" she grumbled good-naturedly when he made room and pulled her back toward the center of the mattress.

His face above hers was sober and sincere. "Not lately, no."

Those few words relieved her much more than she wanted to admit as he slung a long, hairy leg over her thighs and drew her closer.

"As a matter of fact. Not for a very long time." He hesitated then, his blue eyes probing. "And you. Has anyone suggested that you lay claim to your own side of the sheets very nicely, Ms. Adams?"

She held his gaze, knowing he deserved an answer, feeling compelled to give him one. "Only one. And it's been a long time for me, too."

Over a year, in fact, she calculated. While it had been only six months since she'd shared her co-op with Rolfe, it had been much longer since she'd let him share her bed.

She didn't want to think about Rolfe now. Forcing his memory from her mind, she focused on Blue.

He was truly beautiful as he smiled down at her, his expression rich and warm and open. She stretched up and touched her mouth to his. "What was it you wanted to show me?" she asked huskily as her hand drifted to his chest, then wandered lower.

He laughed, retrieved her questing hand and gave her a scolding scowl. "Something you haven't already seen tonight. Something you'll always remember."

"I'll always remember *that*." Her catlike smile had him groaning before he kissed her quickly and rose from the bed.

Offering a hand, he tugged her up with him. "Grab your robe and slip on some shoes."

"What? Why?"

"No questions," he insisted as he pulled up his jeans and toed on his deck shoes. "Hurry, or we'll miss it." His words were muffled beneath his sweatshirt as he dragged it over his head.

"This better be good," she grumbled as she wrapped her robe around her and hunted up a pair of shoes.

Coming to her side, he pulled her flush against him. "I thought you'd decided to trust me."

"That was before I accepted that you were certifiably insane. What kind of a man drags a woman out of a warm bed at...two in the morning?" she groused when she brought his wrist close to her face and checked his watch. "Are you really going to make me go outside?"

"You're whining."

She yawned sleepily and dove for the bed. "Your fault."

Laughing, he hauled her upright again. "Come on. I promise, you won't be sorry. And you know how I feel about promises."

Hershey raised his head from his perch on the sofa when they passed by. Apparently he decided he wasn't up for any nocturnal adventures and laid it back down with a lazy groan.

"I'm with you, Hersh."

"Oh, no you don't." Blue laughed and waylaid her attempted detour back to the sofa, where she intended to curl up on the other end. Tucking her under his arm for security, he walked her toward the door.

They stepped out onto the deck, greeted by a sweet night breeze and an unearthly iridescent glow.

Suddenly awake and wary, she balked when he would have led her down the deck steps. "What *is* that?"

"That," he said, coaxing her gently with him, "is a major miracle of nature. That," he continued with an expansive lift of his hand to the heavens as they cleared the cover of trees and stood under an umbrella of surreal and dazzling color, "is what I didn't want you to miss. Aurora borealis at its brilliant best."

Enthralled, Maggie gazed toward the sky in wonder and awe. "Northern lights."

He wrapped an arm around her shoulder as they looked skyward. "Now are you glad I woke you up?"

She was stunned, completely and totally mesmerized by the beauty of the mysterious phenomenon. Shimmering ethereal columns of reds and greens and blues of varying hues bled color to color in jagged vertical rainbow columns across the midnight Minnesota sky. "I'd only heard about them. I never realized how beautiful they were. And I thought they only occurred in winter."

"Definitely more often in the winter, but occasionally we get a light show up here this time of year. Come on. Let's walk out on the dock and get a better look."

J.D. was drawn to the wonder in Maggie's eyes as she stood there, her neck arched, her gaze cast skyward, her dark eyes reflecting the aurora, the moonlight and her pleasure.

"What causes it?"

"Does it matter?" he asked softly. "A true romantic doesn't care what causes it. A true romantic simply enjoys it."

"And you're a true romantic, aren't you, Blue?"

The sadness in her voice tore at him. Someone had taken her ability to believe in romance away from her. He was determined to give it back, to dispel the shadows of doubt and make her believe again.

"A hopeless romantic," he confessed. "Give me an old Cary Grant movie and I'm in heaven. Give me moonlight and I'm putty in your hands."

"And give you northern lights?"

"Give me northern lights and I take it as a sign that I've got more than enough reason to believe in romance."

His gaze sought hers in the dazzling light show. Sought, and probed and wondered if she would ever open up to him completely.

Someday. Someday, he was determined she would. But not tonight. Tonight, he just wanted to please her.

"You're right," she murmured, turning her gaze back to the sky. "Something this wonderful shouldn't be questioned. It should be enjoyed. Thank you, Blue. Thank you for showing it to me. It's beautiful."

"*You're* beautiful." He wrapped her in his arms from behind and pulled her close. She was softness and substance and the renewed source of his strength. And in this moment, he wondered how he'd gotten by so long in his life without her. "And thank you for coming back to the lake so I could share it with you. I'm damn glad I found you again, Stretch."

A deep breath eased through her slight body as she leaned back against him, covering the arms he'd twined around her waist with hers. "Me, too," she murmured, then tilted her head back and around so she could see his face. "Me, too."

He kissed her then. There on the dock, with the night breeze embracing them and the northern lights shining down. With the sense of being embraced by the forces of nature and a sense of completeness he'd never before known.

"Come on," he whispered gruffly. "Let's go back to bed."

She turned in his arms, stopping him when he would have headed for the cabin. A warm, inviting light danced in her eyes.

His desire was eclipsed only by his love for her sense of adventure when he realized what she had in mind. A slow, pleased smile tipped up one corner of his mouth. "Here?"

"Here," she confirmed, coming up on her tiptoes to whisper a slow, enticing kiss across his lips as she reached for the hem of his sweatshirt. "Now."

The first pale light of the morning sun gilded the bare back of the man sprawled on his stomach sound asleep in her bed. And as she watched him, sleepy yet sated from a night of sweet, thrilling loving, Maggie was afraid she could let herself fall in love.

She should have felt more panicked. But it was getting harder and harder to remind herself that she couldn't afford to let love happen. Not after a lifetime of learning the hard way that love was nothing more than an illusion. Lasting love, at any rate. From family. Between a man and a woman. She knew firsthand that denying that belief meant losing herself in dependency, degrading herself in need. She'd never intended to let herself fall into that trap again.

Yet as she watched her lover sleep, her intentions crumbled like dust in the wind. Blue Hazzard hadn't given a hoot about her intentions. And now she was coming close to not giving a hoot about them, either.

"How did this happen?" she murmured in weary frustration as she lay back beside him and stared toward the ceiling for answers. Instead of answers, she got memories. Memories that reminded her why she was here and why she was a fool to have let herself get so involved.

No one had ever guessed the lie she had lived with Rolfe Sebastion. No one had ever known she was little more than a prisoner of Rolfe's making.

She'd been seventeen when she'd moved to New York. Full of high hopes but no prospects, she'd been waiting tables and scurrying from one cattle call to another with dreams of making it as an actress when Rolfe Sebastion discovered her. The most acclaimed fashion photographer in the States had taken her under his wing as his student, his protégée, his favorite model. And when she'd turned eighteen, he'd made her forget all about her dreams of Broadway when he took her as his lover.

She wiped away a tear that pooled in her eye as she thought back to how easily he'd woven her into his web. Life as she'd known it had been an unending cycle of deprivation and neglect. Except for the Snyders, Rolfe was the first person to offer her an alternative. He'd developed her; he'd nurtured her; he'd enchanted her. Enchantment had turned reluctantly to disillusion, disillusion to painful despair as Rolfe's nurturing degenerated over the years to demands—demands that had grown ugly and manipulative and as controlling as the sex that she'd mistaken for too long as love.

A determined tear escaped, trickling down her cheek and falling to the pillow. She'd thought he loved her. She'd been wrong.

And here she was again, deeply embroiled and deeply caring for another man. She turned her head to look at Blue. He was a man who was so unlike Rolfe it gave her new hope. A man who would, nonetheless, break her heart when he found out how weak she was, then leave her, in disgust, because of it.

But not today. He was not going to leave her today. She dried her eyes, giving in to the pleasure she found in his company. She wasn't ready to let him go. Maybe she wouldn't even be ready next week, she admitted, shamed by her greed but too needy to let him and the joy he brought her go just yet. Not just yet.

Eight

When summer smiles in Minnesota, it's with dazzling blue skies, crisp, clean air and a seductive heat rivaled only by the warmth J.D. felt as he watched Maggie.

He'd tied the Cessna to the dock and was standing on a float, alternately working on the engine and watching her and Hershey play on the beach. She stood knee deep in the water, wearing that neon blue swimsuit that hugged her body like he wanted to. The wind played with her shining chestnut hair; the July sun kissed the honeyed silk of her skin. And his heart melted a little more when she laughed as Hershey bounded around like a pup, begging her to throw a piece of driftwood into the water for him to fetch.

He turned back to the Cessna, knowing he was grinning like a goon and not caring a whit that he was. Just as he was loving every minute of loving Maggie.

The week since they'd first made love had been like an unending scene from every romantic movie he'd ever seen. They were Meg Ryan and Tom Hanks on the top of the

Empire State Building. They were Bogey and Bacall on the edge. They'd made love by moonlight, skinny-dipping and giggling like kids, then collapsing like ancients, completely worn from the exertion.

One day he'd taken her berry picking in the hills where the wild blueberries grew in scattered foot-high clumps. They'd tiptoed around the bear signs, picked and ate their fill of the plump, juicy fruit and ended up making love there, then teasing each other mercilessly when he'd sported stained elbows and knees and she'd come away with a blotched purple bottom. Teasing had turned to loving again when they'd scrubbed each other clean in a long, steamy shower infused with hot sultry kisses.

The memory had him closing the engine cowling, taping it shut and wiping his hands on a grease rag as Maggie's laughter bubbled on the wind again when Hershey barreled into the water after the driftwood like an out-of-control torpedo.

He couldn't remember when he'd been a happier man. Couldn't remember a woman who had ever given him more. Except for one thing. Maggie shared her body and her spirit and her delightful sense of play without holding back. But her past, her deepest thoughts, her feelings for him, she guarded like Hershey guarded his favorite bone.

Time, he reminded himself as he hiked the distance to the beach to join her. *Time and patience and someday she'll trust you enough to share.*

"You have no shame. No shame at all," he scolded as he hit the beach and gathered her in his arms.

She laughed up into his eyes. "What?"

"You know I'm a sucker for those legs, Stretch. And here you are, parading around in that skimpy little suit, showing more legs than a turkey at Thanksgiving. It's hard on a man, I tell you, and you ought to be ashamed."

She draped her wrists around his neck and leaned back into the circle of his bare arms. "A turkey at Thanksgiving? You really do need to work on your lines, Hazzard."

He shared her playful smile. "I thought that by now you'd have realized I'm a man of action not words. But," he added, lifting her into his arms and walking into the water, "I guess maybe you need a reminder."

She laughed. "I hate to break this to you, but in case you haven't noticed, I'm the one in the swimsuit here. You're the one who's getting your jeans wet."

"Oh, I noticed the suit all right." His gaze prowled the length of her bare legs and the soft swell of her breasts pressing against the deep V of fabric that dipped between them. "And unless you want me to strip it off of you in front of Hershey and any ogling fisherman who happens to troll by, I need a little cooling-off period."

She threaded her fingers through the hair at his nape, playing with it. "You *always* need a cooling-off period."

He stopped, thigh deep in the lake, and cocked a brow. "Is that a complaint?"

"Actually...no," she said with a coy little look. "I think maybe it's a compliment."

He snorted. "So...already I'm reduced to a sex object."

One delicate hand, fingers splayed wide, trailed down his bare chest and caressed. "And you love it."

"Yeah, I love it," he growled, lowering his mouth to hers to steal a quick, hot kiss. "But that doesn't mean I don't intend to make you pay." With an ornery grin, he dipped her bottom in the cold water.

She squirmed out of his arms with a laughing squeal and swam away from him. A half beat later, he dove in after her. Hershey joined the fun that turned into a full-fledged water battle and ended with J.D. coaxing Maggie to stand on his shoulders and dive off.

When they were pleasantly exhausted, they stretched out on the beach to dry out in the midmorning sun.

J.D. turned on his side to face her, propping his head on his palm. "It's time, you know."

"Time?" she murmured lazily. "Time for what?"

He ran a finger from the bottom of her chin, down her throat and stopped just short of where fabric met wet flesh between her breasts. "Time for the ultimate test of trust."

She shaded her eyes with her hand and stole a wary glance at him. He wasn't too thrilled about the look that darkened her face. Neither was he thrilled about having to constantly skirt the questions he wanted to ask about her past and her life and why she didn't feel comfortable trusting him with it. But he'd gotten her this far. Far enough, he suspected, that she might just be falling in love with him. Far enough that he didn't want to back her into a corner and scare her off.

"You know you can't put it off any longer, Stretch," he said with mock sternness. "It's time for you to come to terms with the *other* love of my life. It's time you trust me enough to come fly with me."

A look hovering somewhere between relief and horror flitted across her face. Her gaze strayed warily to the Cessna then returned to his, full of determination and denial.

"I'm *not* going up in that thing."

He only smiled.

An hour later, she had changed into pink shorts and a white T-shirt and was sitting in the shotgun seat, Hershey having good-naturedly given it over to her for a spot in the back. After sputtering about the duct tape holding the dated cloth upholstery together, she repeated her mantra for the hundredth time since he'd started his coaxing, cajoling and sweet-talking.

"I'm *not* going up in this thing."

For the hundredth time, he ignored her. Very calmly he fastened her seat belt. "Now, let's go over this again. If I thought for a moment you or I were in any danger, I'd never ask you to fly with me. The plane is old, Maggie, but she's not inoperable. She's a beautiful vintage piece of machinery."

She glared at him.

"So she's a little old. That only makes her better. They just don't make 'em to last like this these days. But if it will make you feel better, even though she's a 1956 model, inside is a newer engine. In fact, FAR—Federal Aviation Regulations," he clarified when her scowl deepened, "requires that the engine be replaced every fifteen hundred hours. This engine only has a little over a thousand hours on it."

She gripped the door handle on one side and the armrest on the other. Focusing first on the yoke directly in front of her that was a twin to his, then on the duct tape holding a cockpit's version of a glove compartment closed, she stared straight ahead. "I'm *not* going up in this thing."

Undaunted, he kept up his babble to soothe her as he pushed the fuel mix button, turned on the key and flipped the motor switch. Watching her face, he engaged the starter, gripped the throttle and gave the plane fuel.

"We'll taxi into the wind," he shouted after the engine had sputtered to life. "There'll be a nice crosswind once we get out of the bay. About fifteen knots, I'd guess. Perfect lift."

"I'm not going up in this thing."

He grinned over at her, noticed her white-knuckled grip and kept up his slow, soothing monologue. "We need about a thousand feet of water for a runway. There's more than enough here, on a nice, glassy surface. Takeoff speed is only around sixty miles per hour—no sweat, right? Once we get airborne we'll cruise at about one-twenty."

"I'm not... Oh...my...God..." Her words drifted off on a rising note and a breathless little whoosh as the Cessna gained speed, J.D. pulled back the yoke and they took flight as gracefully as a Canadian goose set on migration.

"Open your eyes, Maggie," he shouted with a laugh when he turned and saw she had squeezed them so tightly shut he was afraid he'd need a crowbar to open them up. "Enjoy the ride."

"Enjoy? I am *not* going to enjoy this! Blue, please, I don't want to die."

"You're not going to die," he insisted with a gentle smile. "I'd never let that happen. But you're definitely going to miss the scenery if you don't loosen up. Come on, Stretch. Where's that brave, battling wildcat who used to always be ready to take a dare?"

He was starting to feel some real concern that she wouldn't be able to overcome her fear enough to relax. Even more, he was beginning to feel a dark and brooding anger toward whatever—or, more precisely, *who*ever—had doused the fire in her soul and dampened her spirit of adventure.

Carefully holding the Cessna on a straight flight path, he throttled up to one hundred miles per hour and climbed slowly to eight hundred feet, thanking the gods for a low barometer reading, which meant fair winds and smooth flying.

"Weren't you supposed to file a flight pattern or something?"

He angled a look her way, relieved to see she'd opened her eyes and was reluctantly braving a few darting glances out the window.

"Nah. Not up here. The air traffic is limited to float planes and an occasional small charter. At this altitude, I'd see any plane long before it got close enough to cause a problem. Besides, other than my plane, only Red Soldiers hires out, and his bird is in for repairs."

"Why are we shaking?"

"Relax, Maggie. This is not a car. The engine sound alone—not to mention the wind—causes vibrations. All is well. I promise. Please trust me on this."

The mention of his promise seemed to help. So did his appeal for trust. She let out a deep, if shaky breath and loosened her grip on the armrest.

"Are you cold?" he asked when he noticed she'd wrapped an arm around her waist. "I can drop a little lower. The temperature dips a little the higher we climb."

"No, I'm fine . . . relatively speaking," she added in a feeble but game attempt at a grin.

"That's my girl. Now, please, quit worrying and enjoy the sights. Not everyone gets a chance to see the lake like this."

Slowly, Maggie made herself relax. Slower still, she convinced herself she was being foolish. Blue's words— *Where's that brave, battling wildcat who used to always be ready to take a dare?*—had hit the mark. In truth, they'd pierced it, sunk deep and, while he hadn't intended them to, had twisted painfully.

It was difficult to admit that somewhere along the line, in addition to being reduced to a woman whose heart occasionally stopped at shadows in daylight and whose mind sometimes twisted night sounds into night fright, she'd become afraid to live. Rolfe had done that to her.

But she wasn't with Rolfe now. She was with Blue. In the sunlight, in the pure air. In the sweet, safe comfort of his promises.

It hit home suddenly that she was dangerously close to trusting him with her life. A life she was beginning to believe could be rich and full and safe.

Above anything else, that's what she wanted. To feel safe. To feel anchored. That's why she'd come here in the first place. She'd wanted to return to this northwoods setting, where she'd been truly loved; it represented the best part of her past and the only part of her present worth preserving.

And as she rode the air currents of this brilliant summer sky with Blue so dazzlingly handsome and self-assured beside her, she allowed herself to think that the very best might have just begun.

She let out a deep breath and knew that because of him, she could overcome her fear. Not just of going out on a limb and flying in his Cessna, but of living, of always expecting the worst.

Overcoming her fear felt good. But to experience that fear turning to tolerance and then, most unexpectedly, to a sizzling excitement and a warm and wondrous pleasure was something else. Blue, as usual, was right. It was wonderful up here. And she realized with elation that she was enjoying the ride.

The lake country was beautiful from any angle, but from above, it took on another dimension of vast, untamed elegance and wild, unprecedented magnitude.

"I recognize that look."

She turned to him when his voice broke into her thoughts. "What look?"

"The one that says you're about to eat your words for lunch."

She fought a smile. "And what words might those be?"

"Oh, I think they went something like, 'I'm not going to enjoy this.'"

She conceded with a grin even though he looked entirely too pleased with himself. "I was getting a little hungry anyway."

He chuckled and turned his attention back to the plane.

"Thank you," she said, placing a hand lightly on his arm.

He only smiled, looking both pleased and relieved, then turned back to the business of flying.

"Do we have a destination in mind?" she asked a few minutes later as they cruised the skies over hundreds of acres of blue-water bays that trailed like long, spidery fingers into the jagged shoreline of timber and rock.

"Since you said you were hungry, I thought I'd treat you to something special."

When she pressed for more information, he only shook his head. "You'll just have to wait and see."

Fifteen minutes later, Blue set the Cessna gently down in a narrow inlet, then taxied to a huge dock that materialized out of the wilderness like an oasis in the desert. Several boats of various sizes and shapes were moored along the dock's bumpered sides.

"Where are we?"

"The honest-to-goodness last frontier. Crimson Falls."

The moment he shut down the engine she could hear the distant roar of water rushing over rock and wondered if there could actually be a waterfall nearby.

Before she could ask, Blue broke into a broad grin and waved at a pretty teenage girl who was jogging down a grassy slope.

Brown as a berry from hours spent in the sun, the petite strawberry blonde, dressed for July in a bright yellow tank top, short worn cutoffs and bare feet, ran the length of the dock, grabbed the tip of the Cessna's wing and held her steady against the backwash of water that bumped her against the pilings.

Blue shouldered open the cockpit door. "Hey, Casey. How's my one true love?" he teased, tossing out a rope.

Casey's laughing brown eyes and tanned face beamed as she dropped to her knees, batted the single thick braid of red-blond hair behind her back and latched on to the rope.

"Thanks, sweetheart," Blue said when she tied a perfect sailor's knot and made the Cessna fast. "Best dock-side service on the lake."

"About time you showed your ugly face around here again, J. D. Hazzard."

Maggie grinned as Blue managed to look wounded. "Ugly? Is that any way to talk to your own personal heart-throb?"

"In your dreams," Casey bantered back, then squealed in delight when J.D. jumped to the dock, caught her in a growling bear hug, then threatened to throw her in the drink.

"You big bully," she groused on a giggle when he set her down. Then she slugged him in the arm for good measure and giggled again when he clutched his injured limb and staggered in pretended pain.

"You're a cruel woman, Casey Morgan," he muttered darkly.

She made a great show of ignoring him and turned to Hershey. "Now here's *my* kind of guy." Kneeling, she wrapped her arms around an adoring Hershey, whose tail was batting the wooden planks like a pile driver. "Hey, big fella. How's my favorite chocolate dog in the whole wide world?"

"I brought a friend, Case," Blue said as he helped Maggie out of the plane. "Casey, meet Maggie. Maggie... Casey, the heartbreak queen of Crimson Falls."

Suddenly shy when faced with a new woman whose importance to J.D. was as yet undetermined, Casey stood and smiled cautiously. "Hi."

"Hi, yourself." Maggie returned her smile. "And may I say I truly appreciate a woman who knows how to push all the right buttons on the wrong kind of man."

"All right, all right," Blue muttered, doing a pretty good job of playing the wronged male. "Enough with your feminine festival of Hazzard bashing. Take us to your mother, Casey. Deflecting all this bad-mouthing has given me an appetite."

With that auspicious speech behind them, he draped a companionable arm over each of their shoulders. Amid more digs and laughs and inquiries, the three of them, with Hershey trotting happily in and out of the woods, trooped the mile-long path to what Maggie was soon to discover was the Crimson Falls Hotel.

Built at the turn of the century to accommodate loggers and fur traders of the era, the old two-story hotel was a beautiful relic of a past full of history. Though the original grandeur shone through the sagging floors and cracked plaster, Casey's mother, Scarlett Morgan, was obviously struggling to run the hotel as a wilderness retreat on a shoestring budget, a fervent wish and a much-repeated prayer.

"So, how's your burger?" Scarlett asked as she wiped her hands on an apron and joined J.D. and Maggie at one of a dozen old claw-foot oak tables gracing a dining room half full of people.

"It's wonderful," Maggie answered sincerely as she covertly studied the pretty strawberry blonde whose daughter so resembled her in appearance and action. "It's been so long since I've eaten anything but fish, I'd forgotten how satisfying a hamburger could be. I'd also forgotten the wonderful decadence of french fries. *Real* french fries," she added with a blissful sigh.

Scarlett smiled and sat back, openly studying Blue. "So, how's life been treating you, J.D.?"

Maggie ducked her head, pretending to be engrossed in her meal. She had not only liked Scarlett Morgan instantly, she admired the grit it must take to tackle a business as demanding as the northwoods hotel and restaurant in a spot so isolated that the only way to reach it in fair weather was by plane or by water, and in the winter, by plane or snowmobile. To tackle it as a single parent with a healthy, vivacious teenager daughter, who, as sweet as she seemed, was nonetheless a teenager, only increased Maggie's admiration.

And here she was, taking on Blue Hazzard to boot. Scarlett didn't pull any punches. Her calmly asked, "So, how's life been treating you, J.D.?" was loaded with enough unpretentious curiosity to launch a satellite.

Undaunted, J.D. dug into his own burger. "My life is just swell, Scarlett. In fact, my life has never been better."

Scarlett gave him a considering look, then cast a red-faced Maggie a knowing smile. "Well, I'm real glad to hear that."

"I'm sure knowing it will make you sleep better," J.D. put in, waiting a beat and adding, "Mother."

Maggie lifted a brow.

"Old joke," Blue clarified. "Scarlett thinks she can mother everyone she meets into happiness. Some people call it meddling. But not me," he added hastily when Scarlett's eyes narrowed. "Not to change the subject, but how's business?"

Scarlett shrugged. "Picking up. It's been a pretty good summer and I've got bookings into September that should make a dent in the overhead."

"I hear a 'but' in there somewhere," Blue added when Scarlett's voice trailed off.

"No buts," she said, in what Maggie recognized as forced brightness. "Everything's fine. Everything's great."

Scarlett rose, effectively closing the door on any more inquiries about business. "Duty calls. I've got to run. It's been really nice meeting you, Maggie. Make sure you talk this sky jockey into bringing you back again sometime. Casey's quite taken with you. And I'd love your company again, too."

"It's been my pleasure," Maggie insisted, meaning it.

"Take care, J.D." Scarlett turned to go but stopped abruptly. "Almost forgot. Have you made any progress on the poachers?"

Maggie watched as Blue's expression darkened. "Nothing. They're strictly hit-and-run. Slippery as oil and just as crude."

"Well, keep at it. Something'll turn up."

"She's charming," Maggie said as she watched Scarlett walk away.

"And gutsy as hell. I worry about her though. She's running this business on a nonexistent profit margin."

"She's a good friend?"

He nodded. "And she's had a rough road. Casey's father was—" he paused and worked a muscle in his jaw. "Let's just say he was a fool and Scarlett and Casey have paid the price."

"Something tells me that if anyone can handle tough times, it's those two."

He grinned. "You've got that right. When you're finished," he added, turning his full attention back to her, "there's something I want to show you before we head back."

What he wanted to show her was the miracle of nature that gave Crimson Falls its name. The falls was a wild and foamy watershed dropping a hundred feet over a rock cliff that reflected sunlight and sparkling spray against iron-rich ore. The result created an optical illusion of crimson ribbons cascading in spectacular, tumbling glory to the depths of the rapids below.

"It's incredible." She had to shout to be heard above the water's roar.

"So are you," he said, turning her in his arms. He brushed a strand of wind-teased hair from the corner of her mouth. "So are you."

His kiss was as warm as the sun, yet as full of power as the falls rumbling the ground beneath their feet.

"I like your friends," she said against his chest when he pulled her companionably against him. "Especially in light of the fact that they recognized me—I saw Casey showing her mother an old copy of *Glamour*—and didn't make a fuss.''

"That's because in addition to being wowed by you, they liked you, too. *I* like you," he added.

"Well that works out real nice, because I like you too," she said after the long moment it took to work up her courage.

It was a first for her. The first time she'd tested the waters and let herself respond in kind.

Everything had been so perfect between them these past few weeks. She knew he cared about her. And while he'd made noises about believing in love at first sight, he hadn't forced the issue again. For that she was thankful. Until today, she hadn't wanted to chance ruining what they had with words neither could own up to.

Today was different. Chalk it up to the adrenaline high of her death-defying flight in Blue's beloved plane. Until today, she hadn't been brave enough to let herself sort through her feelings when it came to Blue. Feelings, she was beginning to suspect, that would lead her straight into a relationship where she'd grow to depend on and love him.

That was the scary part. She'd been there. She'd done that. She was feeling the residual pain and humiliation of it to this day. That's why it was so hard to get to this point, to thinking in terms of giving herself over to Blue. Anyone she'd ever loved had let her down. If it happened again, if it happened with Blue, she wasn't sure she had it in her to recover another time.

"It's time we head back," he said, his words breaking into thoughts she was more than happy to shake off.

"Unless you want to get a room," he suggested with a wiggle of his brows and a suggestive leer. "I think we could talk Scarlett into renting one by the hour. Especially in light of the fact that the hotel used to be a brothel."

His playful suggestion and the mention of the brothel surprised her out of her melancholy. "No kidding?"

"So the story goes."

"I think I want to hear this story."

On the way back to the Cessna he filled her in on a history as rich and rowdy as the trappers and loggers who had stopped at the hotel in the late 1800s and early 1900s to slake their thirst in the hotel's bar, curb their hunger in the welcoming dining room and satisfy other, more carnal appetites in the rooms upstairs.

"Crimson Falls is even rumored to have a ghost," he added with a grin that was as suspicious as it was disarming.

"Ghost?"

"A soiled dove who was jilted at the altar. The story is that she's roamed the halls of the hotel for almost a hundred years looking for her runaway bridegroom."

"No man is worth that kind of vigil," she commented with a sniff of conviction.

"Not even a man who..." His voice trailed off as he tucked her under his arm and whispered in vivid, shocking detail what he had planned for her tonight when he got her alone in her bed.

"Well," she said, feeling herself redden with both the heat of embarrassment and the thrill of unmentionable pleasures, "I may have been a little hasty. Any man who can..." She stopped, swallowed, then tilted a wide-eyed skeptical frown up at him. "You can really do that?"

He nodded smugly and her knees went as wobbly as her heartbeat.

"Then I've got one thing to say to you, Hazzard."

"And that is?"

"Prove it."

That night, in the dark, in her bed, in a silence suspended only by sultry sighs, the rustle of sheets and her soft, shuddering moans of pleasure, he proved he was a

man of his word . . . and that she just might be a woman
capable of holding a vigil.

"Are you ready, Stretch?"

"Are you sure this is such a good idea?"

"Chickening out on me?"

She sucked in a deep, determined breath and gave him a
look. "Just offering you one last out."

"She's all yours, Amelia."

Maggie reached forward and grasped the yoke in front of
her. The minute Blue let go of his and gave over control of
the plane to her, she experienced a moment of stark, un-
adulterated horror that took everything in her to fight off.

"'At a girl." Blue's voice purred across the cockpit, offering assurances, turning over his trust. "You're a natural."

She didn't feel like a natural. She felt like a tense mass of
nerves who had finally tipped over the far side. She was
eight hundred feet in the air, in control—loosely speaking—of an airplane that barely looked like it could float, let
alone fly.

It was her third flight in as many days. And unlike the
first time, when Blue had done the badgering, she was the
one who had wheedled him into taking her up today.

Like her affinity for the lake, the thrill of riding the wind
currents in the small aircraft had gotten in her blood, too.
She wanted to experience it all—the tummy-tumbling ex-
hilaration of the takeoff, the sweet freedom of flight, the
risky bump and glide of a rough water landing. And when,
on impulse, Blue had offered to let her pilot the plane, she
hadn't had it in her to say no.

"You're doing fine," he crooned in her ear. "If you want
to increase altitude, just pull the yoke toward you. That's
it. Good. Not too fast. Better. Much better. See? I told you
you could do it."

The Cessna tipped suddenly to the right.

"What's happening?" she demanded with wild-eyed urgency.

"Stay cool. You're fine. We just hit an air pocket. See that little bubble on the instrument panel? Try to keep it in the middle. Just turn the yoke to the left a bit...a little more. Hold it. All better, see? It's just that simple."

There was nothing simple about it and she knew it. But she thanked him with a quick glance, telling him how special she thought he was for letting her think she was in control. There wasn't a cloud in the sky, not an obstacle in view, and any damage she could do, he could rectify with little fuss.

"Bank left for me, Stretch. That's it. Nice and wide. I saw something down there I want to get a better look at."

The Cessna responded prettily to her maneuvering and she realized, with something that rivaled the excitement of making love with Blue, why he was in love with flying.

"Your turn," she offered gravely, deciding she'd tested her wings long enough for her first trip out.

"You're sure you've had enough?"

She nodded.

He gave her a quick kiss of congratulations then took over the controls. "You did great—for a rookie."

She felt great, too.

"How would you feel about an unscheduled stop?"

They'd already flown to Crane Cove, where she'd met some of his friends and fueled up the plane. Now they were on their way back to Blue Heron Bay and home.

"What'd you have in mind?"

"See that bay down there?"

She recognized it immediately. "That's *my* bay."

"Now look over the other wing. There's a log cabin on the far shore."

She strained and just barely made out the roofline of the structure he was referring to.

"I see it."

"That's your friend Greene's place."

"Really?" She looked the spot over with more interest. "I didn't realize he lived that far from me."

"It's not really that far. Not by water. Want to pay him a visit?"

She frowned, hesitating. Abel was an extremely private man. She didn't feel comfortable dropping in unannounced.

"It's probably not a good idea. He hasn't exactly made himself visible the last few weeks."

He gave her a knowing smile. "That's because he knows I've been taking up your time."

"How could he know that?"

His smile turned brooding. "He knows. Trust me. He knows."

Despite the fact that she voiced her reservations again, Blue took the Cessna in for a smooth water landing. As they settled down, Maggie told herself there was no reason for the taste of unease that had begun to rise in her throat like sour milk. Blue's only reason for stopping was to give her the opportunity to see Abel. He was not using her to provide himself with an opportunity to do a little impromptu investigating that might implicate Abel in the poaching crimes.

Unease was replaced by guilt. How could she even think it? She knew Blue better than that. He deserved better from her. This man, whom she had trusted with her body, with her life, and was dangerously close to trusting with her heart, was not about to put that trust at risk and disappoint her.

Nine

Maggie sat tensely as Blue taxied the plane into a shallow bay. A narrow dock harbored a small fishing boat and a canoe on one side. The float plane just fit on the other.

"It doesn't look like he's home," she said with a wary look toward the shore when Blue cut the motor.

But for the water sounds and the bird song and the July breeze whispering through the trees, all was quiet. As quiet as a church during a funeral. As still as the eye of a storm.

She wasn't sure why those particular analogies came to mind. Neither was she sure why she'd made such a rapid emotional descent from the exhilarating high of her first piloting experience to this sick feeling of deepening dread.

"Coming here was a mistake," she said, in a last-ditch effort to persuade Blue she wanted to leave.

"We're here, Maggie." His smile relayed confusion over her hesitance. "It's a little too late to leave without announcing ourselves, don't you think?"

"Maybe he's not home."

"I thought you'd like to see him," Blue said, looking genuinely puzzled.

"His boat's here," he added, when her silence was her only response. Easing out of the cockpit, he tied up to the dock. "He can't be far away."

Slowly, she joined him on the dock, shading her eyes against the late-afternoon sun as she searched the lake-shore for signs of Abel.

No Trespassing signs were posted in multiple and con-spicuous spots—at the end of the dock, again at the point where dock met shore, on the birch and aspen lining the bank.

"I don't think he wants to be bothered," she whispered, as if she were in a library and afraid to bring down the wrath of a temperamental librarian.

"I don't think the warnings were meant to discourage friends." His staged whisper mimicked hers. He grinned when she scowled at him. "The trouble with owning prop-erty on this lake is that vacationing fishermen have a ten-dency to make themselves at home if they see a welcoming dock and an absentee owner. The signs are just a form of protection from unwanted visitors. Now come on."

He took her hand and led her up the narrow planks to-ward shore, her unease thickening. Even Hershey, whose usual exuberance would have had him barreling toward the woods in search of a chippy to chase, tiptoed ahead of them, slow and wary.

Her reservations multiplied with each step. A question she didn't want to entertain kept crashing her thoughts like a battering ram. Why had Blue decided to stop? He'd told her once that in all his travels of the lake, he'd never paid Abel a visit. Why today? A niggling and relentless voice—the voice of experience that reminded her how she'd been used in her life—kept warning her it was because she was his admission ticket.

By the time they reached the steps of stone that led up the sloping path to his log cabin, however, her hesitancy gave way to a curious fascination as she took in Abel Greene's private domain.

Abel went to extreme measures, it seemed, to not only live in nature, but to commune with it. Towering Norwegian pine grew in such close proximity to a massive log cabin that she wondered how he'd managed to build it among them. He'd taken special care not to disturb the huge, gnarled roots that extended out of solid rock like crooked, arthritic fingers. Every twisted claw that bent back in on itself had been filled with soil and planted. Wild iris, baby strawberries, sweet williams, nodding columbines and a dozen other varieties Maggie recognized but couldn't name filled the mini flower beds, becoming one with the forest floor, enhancing the natural drama of the landscape.

"It's beautiful," she whispered, her awe overriding the last of her trepidation. "Look." She nodded to a spot farther up the slope. "Listen."

The exotic and elusive sound of wind chimes had drawn her attention, as well as the multitude of bird feeders catering to everything from hummingbirds, to chickadees, to finches, and a dozen other varieties that flitted from one to the other even as they stood there watching.

"What is that?" She pointed to a spot farther from the cabin.

Blue drew his brows together. "A salt lick. Deer love 'em. That's a mineral block beside it. And from the looks of things, they like the corn he must feed them, too."

Telltale corn chaff and deer tracks littered the ground, lending credence to Blue's conclusion.

"The man grows flowers, feeds birds and deer, hangs wind chimes," she said expansively, then voiced aloud the thought that had been hammering at her. "How could anyone suspect him of being involved with anything as hideous as poaching bear?''

She turned to Blue, her conviction firm, until she saw the look on his face. It was a look that made her blood chill by degrees.

"Sonofabitch," he swore under his breath as his gaze locked on a spot past hers.

With a weary breath and a grim set of his mouth, he walked over to a shed that was built into a rock wall. When he reached it, he hunkered down to get a better look at whatever it was that had drawn him there.

Maggie's heart hit her ribs like a rock fired from a slingshot. "What?" she asked anxiously, following him as he examined the barrel-shaped apparatus partially hidden under a canvas tarp beside the shed.

"What is it?" she insisted, coming up behind him, her footsteps muffled by the moss and pine needles blanketing the forest floor.

Blue didn't answer her. Abel did.

"It's a live bear trap."

Maggie and Blue spun as one toward the sound of Abel's voice. Hershey made a whining noise deep in his throat, the hair on his back trying to bristle in the moment before he spotted the wolf dog, Nashata, by Abel's side.

Maggie sucked in a sharp breath, her hand flying to her throat. "Abel. My God. You scared me half to death."

He didn't speak. He just stared at her, his eyes darkened with what she recognized as disappointment and betrayal.

"I'm a little surprised myself," he said finally, and let Nashata go to Hershey, who was now gamely wagging his tail. "Surprised to find you here, that is."

Filled with feelings of guilt for intruding, her smile was forced. "Blue thought it might be nice to pay you a visit."

Abel's gaze swung to Blue's and locked. A muscle flexed in his jaw as he gave a jerk of his chin and his satin black hair, hanging loose and long about his bare chest, fell back behind his shoulders. "I'll just bet he did. Find what you were looking for, Hazzard?"

Maggie felt a sick, sinking sensation deep in her stomach as she watched the two men's eyes clash.

"I'm sure Abel has an explanation for the trap," she said quickly. Too quickly, her voice defensive, protective and not a little bit pleading as she looked back to Abel for confirmation.

"I'm sure I do," Abel said stiffly. "The problem will be getting anyone to listen."

With a long, hard look at J.D. he turned and walked away.

Torn between a need to go to him and slink away like the snake she felt she was, she just stood and watched him go.

"Come on, Maggie," Blue said, his voice hard as he snagged her arm. "Let's get out of here."

Maggie was unnaturally quiet on the short ride back to her bay. But then, he wasn't much better, J.D. acknowledged grimly as the Cessna glided up to her dock. It was nearly dusk when he eased out of the cockpit and turned to her, offering her a hand out. She ignored it, climbing out of the plane on her own steam. For a moment, all he could do was stand there.

He'd known she was upset. She had every right to be. And he was partially to blame.

Steeped in regret, damning himself for a fool and Greene for disappointing her, he couldn't think how he was going to make it up to her. Because of him, she'd had to face head-on the disappointing possibility that Greene was not the man she thought he was. Because of him, she'd been confronted with some damning evidence that might put Greene behind bars.

"Nice going, Hazzard," he grumbled under his breath. "This trick definitely fits under 'it seemed like a good idea at the time.'"

It *had* seemed like a good idea. He'd gotten a sense over the past few weeks that she'd had a need to see Greene again, if for no other reason than to make sure he was all right. As it turned out, he should have listened to her and not set down.

He saw again the bear trap and the look in Greene's eyes. Yeah, he wanted this poaching business stopped, but not at Maggie's expense. And while Greene had always been a suspect, J.D. really hadn't wanted to find out he was involved. While the presence of the trap wasn't conclusive evidence, it sure as hell pointed a finger straight in his direction.

After making the Cessna fast, he walked the slope to the cabin. Maggie was curled up in a chair by the window, staring out over the bay, her face blank of emotions.

A silence as heavy as his regret hung in the air as he slowly walked to her side. "I'd have done anything to have spared you that."

After a long moment, she met his eyes. The ice in them chilled him to the bone. "Anything but miss the opportunity to take advantage of my friendship with Abel."

The rancor in her tone hit him like a broadside blow from a two-by-four. Before he could collect himself enough to react, she slammed him again.

"I thought you were different. I *counted* on you to be different."

J.D. just stood there, stunned by words made all the more cutting because of the accusation in her eyes, unable to connect with why it was directed at him. He knelt by her chair, then stared at empty air when she rose and deliberately walked away from him.

Something inside him snapped as he watched the rigid, closed-off set of her shoulders. Something deep and elemental that demanded she make sense of her actions and accusations, something that held court to a rapidly building anger.

Jaw set, brows creased, he let out his breath between clenched teeth. Rising, he propped his fists on his hips and stared at her back. "What are you doing?" Panic, coupled with anger, bore down hard. "What the *hell* is this about?"

She turned back to him, the ice in her eyes sullied by a heartbreaking regret. "It's about manipulation. It's about trust. I trusted you. I *trusted* you ... and you used me."

He'd never been in an earthquake. Never experienced the ground rumble and shift and drop out from under him as he stood helpless to let it happen. He felt like he was in one now. Everything that was important to him seemed to crumble beneath his feet and dump him into a deep and unforgiving chasm.

He reacted like a man caught on the edge of disaster with a tight, controlling leash on his emotions, with an unswerving determination to come out of it alive. "I'd like to play this cool, Stretch. I'd like to stand here and take this, tell myself you're upset and let it go. I'd like to ... but right now, I just haven't got it in me." His gaze bore into hers, hard and demanding. "Explain, please, exactly how I ended up the bad guy in all this."

She shook her head, tears glistening. "It was so easy, wasn't it? You knew Abel wouldn't welcome you, so all you had to do was come up with an excuse to take me to see him. Once you got me there, how could you not take advantage of the opportunity to try to catch him in the act?" The hurt in her words was eclipsed only by her conviction. "I don't even know why I'm surprised. I should be used to it by now. Someone has always found a use for me if it meant they could get what they wanted."

He closed his eyes and drew a deep breath. He counted to ten. Then twenty, and was afraid even then that if he didn't go very, very carefully he just might have to hit something—like the wall. And for the first time in his life, he realized he had the capacity to be a violent man.

The force of the discovery rocked him. Blood pounded in his ears as he struggled to regain control and filter through his emotions. With more strength of will than he thought possible, he settled himself down. And he forced himself to see through the anger she directed dead center at him.

He'd sensed the change in her back at Greene's. He'd attributed it to shock. He'd seen the hurt and had read it as disappointment in Abel Greene.

What he hadn't seen—what in retrospect he should have realized—was that the raw, crippling emotion clouding her eyes with accusations of betrayal was not directed at Abel but at him.

He saw it now. She made sure of it. It was all there. Disappointment, clear and cutting. Outrage, pure and perverse.

"You're reaching, Stretch," he said, fighting to keep the anger from his voice. "You're reaching real far."

He swallowed hard, made himself breathe and tipped his head toward the window and a night that seemed bright in comparison to his dark disappointment.

"You know...trust runs both ways. I'm trying very hard right now to trust that this really isn't about me. I'm trying *damn* hard to trust that you've just suffered a major disappointment and since I'm the one who's handy, I'm the one taking the blame."

Her silence filled the room, heavier than stone, as damning as a guilty verdict. He turned back to her, looking for a sign that the truth of his words had reached her. But in that protective gesture she'd used with such regularity in the beginning but which he hadn't seen for weeks now, she crossed her arms tightly beneath her breasts, distancing herself even further.

"What happened to you?" he demanded when she drew further into herself and turned her back on him again.

He wasn't having any of it. He stalked up behind her, gripped her by her shoulders and spun her around, making her confront him. "Who hurt you? Who hurt you so badly that you need to blame me for the damage he's done?"

He let out a deep breath when she stood silent and defensive before him. "Why can't you see that I'm not him?"

Abruptly, he let her go. "Damn you. Damn you, Maggie," he gritted out, unable to bite back his resentment. "You owe me a helluva lot more than stubborn silence."

After a last penetrating look that begged her to confide in him, he swore under his breath and turned away.

He had to get away from her. He had to get away from her now, before he said something he'd regret even more than he regretted her lack of faith in him.

"I can't do this by myself," he said, hearing both the plea and the weariness that he felt. "I can't fix things if you won't tell me what's broken."

When more silence was her only response, he snagged the doorknob and wrenched it open. "I'm outta here." Then he stopped short when Abel Greene's brooding face stared back at him from the other side.

For a moment J.D. couldn't react. He just stood there, working hard on salvaging his bruised pride, working harder on keeping one fist wrapped around the doorknob and the other at his side. Nothing would make him happier than connecting with Greene's granite-hard face just because it happened to be handy—and because he knew it would feel damn good to knock him down.

"What the hell are you doing here?" he snarled.

Greene didn't budge an inch. "The trap," he said, meeting J.D.'s glare, "is for a cub I've heard prowling at night. I think the poachers got its mother. If I can trap it and transport it north, it'll have a fighting chance of surviving."

J.D. squared his shoulders and studied the big man's face. He knew without questioning why that he'd just heard the truth. That didn't mean he was in a mood for expounding on that revelation. "And you came over here in the dark to tell me that."

Greene cast a narrowed glance over J.D.'s shoulder to Maggie before going on. "I came because I found the poacher's camp. Looks like they're planning another hunt. When I spotted activity tonight, I radioed the DNR. Thought you might want to be there when they make the bust."

Greene's stoic, unruffled calm triggered a corresponding calm in J.D. He let out a deep breath. The opportunity to work off his anger by taking part in the downfall of the low-life scum who had been exploiting and wasting a resource as unique and peace-loving as the black bear was exactly what he needed.

"How many and where are they?" he asked, stepping outside, barely aware that Maggie had followed him out the door.

"Three, maybe four men. They're holed up in the Gators."

"The Alligators? Damn. No wonder we couldn't find them."

The Alligators were a maze of islands, the channels in between booby-trapped with humpbacked and razor-sharp rock piles lying just under the water's surface. One wrong maneuver through the series of spines that resembled the reptile that gave them their name and you could rip the bottom out of a boat. Or shear a prop and end up stranded or sunk. Or worse, in rough water, be rammed against the treacherous shoreline. The Gators were Legend Lake's version of the Bermuda Triangle. Only a fool or someone wanting very badly not to be bothered would venture into such dangerous water.

And only someone like Abel Greene, who knew the lake like the back of his hand, would risk searching for the poachers in there. Fortunately for the black bear, his risk had paid off.

"When did you find them?"

"A couple of days ago. I've been watching to make sure I knew what they were up to."

"How long's it going to take us to get to them in your boat?" J.D. asked as they walked hurriedly across the dock.

"An hour maybe. The lake's calm tonight. The DNR'll be about a half hour behind us, providing they can follow my directions and find their way in."

"And just what do you two think you're going to do until they get there?"

Until he heard her voice—and the urgency in it—J.D. hadn't realized that Maggie was scrambling along behind them, listening to every word.

Greene's appearance at her door with news of the poachers had momentarily deflected his attention from her to a more tangible target. Her voice and the worry on her face, however, brought back the immediacy of her accusations and triggered a fresh wave of anger.

"This doesn't concern you, Maggie," he said, his words sounding every bit as hard as he wanted them to be.

"It doesn't concern you either!" she insisted, ignoring him and appealing to Greene. "This is something you should leave to the law. You're not trained to capture dangerous criminals!"

J.D. clenched his jaw, strode to the Cessna and jerked open the cockpit door.

"All the DNR boys asked is that we keep them in sight until they get there," Abel put in, in an attempt to calm Maggie down while J.D. reached into the cockpit and stuffed everything from a flashlight to a pipe wrench to a roll of duct tape into a knapsack.

He handed it down to Abel, who was already in the boat.

"We won't be in any danger," Abel added as J.D. stepped in beside him.

"Then I'm going, too."

"No," J.D. said flatly when she made to scramble in after him. "No way."

"You're not my boss, Hazzard. And neither are you, Abel," she added hastily as she jerked on the sweatshirt she'd snagged on her way out the door. "If you're going, I'm going, and if you dump me out, I'll follow in my own boat."

"You don't know how to run a boat."

She jammed her arms into the sweatshirt and tugged it over her head. "Then it'll be on your head, won't it, if I get lost or drown out there."

J.D. glared from her to Abel.

"We've got to get going, Hazzard. Make the call."

J.D. let out a deep breath, already regretting what he was about to say, but knowing he didn't have time to argue. "All right, dammit. But you stay in this boat when we hit the island and you keep yourself low and quiet, got it?"

She didn't say a word.

"You got it?" he repeated on a near roar, and was rewarded when she flinched, then gave him a sharp, defensive nod before she plunked down beside Hershey, who was already firmly ensconced in the bow.

She avoided his glare when he shoved a life jacket into her hands and ordered her to put it on. He took small comfort when her eyes flared fire, but she did as she was told.

Abel's flat-bottom fishing boat cut through the night waters like a sharp blade slicing through soft butter. Maggie rode with her back to the open lake, silent and more than a little solemn as she watched the two men, their heads bent together, talking strategy above the motor's hum.

She sat in the bow, hugging her arms around herself to ward off the chill of the night wind buffeting her—and the icy, empty look in Blue's eyes when they occasionally strayed her way.

She ached as she watched him and Abel. Abel's proud features were sharpened by night shadows and intensity, the ragged destruction of the scar on his face highlighted by moon glow and determination. He was a man much misunderstood. A lonely man whose integrity was overshadowed only by his mysterious aloofness. A man whose lone-wolf demeanor left him open for accusations and distrust.

And then there was Blue. Blue, whom she had fallen in love with. She was so afraid to admit to that love that she had tried to drive him away tonight. Blue, who had never wanted to believe the worst in Abel, and with a simplicity that shamed her, accepted Abel's explanation about the trap without hesitation. It was an acceptance she suspected Abel had received little of in his life.

And yet she, in retaliation for the actions of another man, hadn't had it in her to accept Blue's motives as simple and pure.

His handsome features were drawn with concentration as the wind batted his blond hair back from his face. The mobile lines of his mouth were tightened with determination and intensity. And never once did he let his gaze fall on her with anything but a cursory glance.

She felt heartsick. When this was over, she'd make it up to him. She'd tell what had happened to her today. She'd explain about the avalanche of emotions that had caught her off guard and triggered a panic so profound that she'd lashed out at him for the sins of everyone who had preceded him in her life. She'd share everything she should have confided to him long before now, everything she'd intended to tell him when she'd realized he was going to walk out her door tonight, before Abel's sudden appearance had stopped her.

Her heart stumbled hard over the thought that she might have blown her chance just as Abel cut the motor.

Silence descended over the small watercraft as the bow nestled deeper into the water, settling with the gentle swell of the rocking waves.

"We go on our own steam from here," Abel whispered, as light as a shadow, through the night breeze. "Our approach was downwind so they couldn't have heard us, but we don't want to take any chances. I spotted a ninety-horse outboard on their tri-hauler. We won't stand a chance in ten of keeping up with them if they decide to cut and run."

"Then maybe we ought to take those big horses out of commission," Blue said with grim intent, his voice as hushed as Abel's.

At his nod of agreement and without further exchange of words, both men lifted paddles from the floor of the boat. Taking deep, silent cuts into the black water, they maneuvered through a maze of channels and humpback rocks toward an island a hundred yards in the distance.

When they were within ten feet of the rocky shore, Blue, with speed and athletic grace, slipped to the bow of the boat. Lowering himself noiselessly over the side, he towed them toward a weedy inlet, beaching the boat quietly.

Abel followed soon after, dragging the bow line with him and tying the boat fast to an uprooted tree that jutted out over the water's edge.

Not for the first time since they'd cast off, Maggie felt a real and immediate fear for both of them. "What exactly are you going to do?" she whispered when Blue again ordered her to stay in the boat with Hershey.

"We're just going to keep an eye on them until the DNR men get here," he whispered brusquely, then cast a telling glance Abel's way.

She recognized that look. It was a look a man gave to another man when what they'd just told a woman was exactly the opposite of what they meant.

Before she could call him on it, they took off with one last order: "No matter what happens, stay in this boat."

Maggie didn't consider herself a particularly brave person— Lord knew, her fear of loving Blue was proof of that. Neither did she consider herself stupid. And as she sat there, shadows blending to stone, stone to timber, and minutes blending into an hour, she didn't for a minute believe she would do anything but hamper Blue and Abel if she were foolish enough to go after them.

For that reason and that reason only, she made herself stay put, her arm around a restless Hershey, whose whining pants together with the slap of water to shore were the only break in the silence of this dark and potentially dangerous night.

"I don't know why they just couldn't have left it to the DNR," she murmured in a hushed whisper, hoping the sound of her voice would calm both her and Hershey. "Because Abel knows he was a suspect and feels he has a right to see his name cleared, that's why, right Hershey? And because Blue, in addition to being in on the search from the beginning and feeling entitled to see it through to the end, also wants to show Abel he trusts him."

Trust. The word fell on her chest like lead. If only she had trusted Blue.

Please, please, please let him get out of this unhurt so I can show him how sorry I am, she prayed in silence to a God she hoped still listened to her.

"They're big boys, Hershey," she went on aloud, fighting another overwhelming urge to go look for him. Casting about for confidence and for more reasons to stay in this boat when the man she loved could be in danger, she expanded her argument. "They can take care of themselves. That was a pretty big wrench Blue tossed in..." Her words trailed off when she spotted the knapsack with the wrench and who knew what else on the floor of the boat.

"Oh, Hersh, Blue forgot the knapsack."

She huddled closer to the lab and scowled toward the dark island, thick with trees and rock and undergrowth and frightening unknowns...and knew she'd just found her reason to go after him.

Ten

"I don't think I'm heroine material," Maggie muttered as she snagged the knapsack from the floor, latched onto Hershey's collar with a death grip and somehow managed to climb out of the boat without making too much noise. At any rate, she hoped she hadn't made much noise. That feat, at least, would make up for the fact that she was wet to her knees and scared down to her soggy soles of what she might find—or of what might find her—as she made her way up the sloping shore and began hiking slowly toward the center of the densely wooded island.

She hadn't tripped over more than twenty yards of undergrowth and rock when she heard voices. Heart pounding, she tightened her grip on Hershey's collar with one hand and the knapsack with the other. Hershey reacted to the sounds with a low, predatory growl.

She dropped to her knees beside him. "Shh. Good dog. Please, please be a good dog and shh," she whispered urgently, afraid the lab would give them away before she figured out if she'd caught up with Blue and Abel or, God forbid, the poachers.

She snuck up a few more feet, peeked out from behind a tree, then smothered a gasp when she spotted a clearing with a camp fire burning in the center. The low rumble of voices—angry voices—became more pronounced, stepping up the rhythm of her heart to a rate she'd never hit in the most strenuous aerobic workout as it sank home that she'd stumbled onto the poacher's camp.

Her self-preservation instincts begged her to turn around and go back, to wait it out and trust Abel and Blue to take care of themselves. But every protective instinct she owned sat up and took over when she heard Blue's voice rise above the muddle of shouted words.

Fear clutched her throat and fisted. Through the cover of night, with the faint light from the fire, she strained to make out the dark shapes of several burly men—and spotted the unmistakable silhouettes of Blue and Abel in the middle of them.

Clinging tight to Hershey's collar, she inched closer. She bit back an involuntary scream when she realized Blue and Abel were surrounded by—her heart kicked hard and fast when she counted—six men. Two of them were pointing the business ends of long-barreled guns directly at Blue and Abel's chests as they stood among them, their hands clasped prayerlike on top of their heads.

One thought dominated all others then. The two men she cared about more than anyone else on this earth were in danger and she had to come up with a plan to help them.

They have guns, her common sense screamed. She didn't know how to deal with guns—just like she didn't know how to deal with complete and total brain lock as panic stole her powers of reason and clear thinking took a hike to Canada. As it turned out, she didn't need a plan anyway. Hershey had one of his own.

She didn't know later if she screamed before or after Hershey lurched toward his master. She only knew that when the dog launched himself, she fell flat on her face and the wind flew out of her body in a hard, agonizing whoosh.

When she'd ridden out the worst of the pain and had drawn the first of several gasping breaths of air, she pushed herself to all fours, shook her head to clear it and took stock.

In one hand, she still had a death grip on the knapsack—in the other she held a broken piece of leather that was Hershey's collar.

"Oh, my God," Maggie breathed as she scrambled to her feet and raked the hair out of her eyes.

All hell had broken loose around the fire. Blue was doing battle with two bearded thugs. One was riding his back. The other came at him with a rifle butt from his blind side. Abel rolled on the ground with one of the poachers, perilously close to the fire, while another one was bearing down hard. And Hershey—sweet, puppy-eyed Hershey—snarling and sniping, wrestled one man to the ground and latched on to his arm like he wouldn't rest until he ripped it out of the socket.

When she saw the sixth man raise his rifle and take aim at Blue, she didn't give cowardice or bravery much thought. She just reacted. She ran headlong into the thick of pounding fists and vicious growls, wielding the knapsack like a war club.

The wrench inside the canvas sack connected with the poacher's head with a resounding crack. He dropped like a stone, never knowing what had hit him.

For a split second, all Maggie could do was stare—first at the fallen man, then at the sack. A sickening rush of nausea swamped her when she realized what she'd done.

"Maggie! The rifle!"

She jerked her head up at the sound of Blue's voice.

"Grab it!" he yelled as he ducked a swinging fist, connected with a solid upper cut to the jaw of the man in front of him, then jammed an elbow into the ribs of the man coming at him from behind.

As frightened as she was for Blue, on some subconscious level she knew he was holding his own, as was Abel, whose actions she caught in her peripheral vision.

Forcing herself to back away from the grisly reality that she might have killed a man, she bent on shaking legs and picked up the gun. She hadn't a clue how to use it. She didn't let that stop her.

"Hershey!" she yelled, straining to be heard above his vicious growls as he attacked the downed man, who was begging her to call him off.

"Hershey!" she commanded more forcefully, until the dog, his lips curled in a feral challenge, his sides heaving with exertion, backed away.

She pointed the rifle directly at the poacher's chest.

"I'm shaking so badly right now," she said in a reed-thin voice, "that any move you make just might make me jerk the finger I have on this trigger. Do you understand?"

He nodded, his face twisted with pain as he clutched his bleeding arm.

"Then you're going to stay right where you are, aren't you?"

Again, he nodded, then doubled over with a groan, pulled his knees to his chest and tucked his injured arm close to his body.

Keeping the gun trained on him, she glanced toward the action around the fire. Two men lay unconscious. The other two hadn't yet figured out that Abel and Blue were pounding the ever-loving daylights out of them and were stupid enough to keep coming back for more.

With a jab to the jaw, Blue laid the last thug low, then stood, legs spread wide, his broad chest heaving. Blood trickled from the corner of his mouth. One eye was swollen and bleeding as he swung his gaze first to Abel, confirming he was in control of his situation. Only then did he turn to Maggie.

Firelight danced across his beautiful, battered face. Blood lust still raced through his veins, darkening his eyes to midnight blue lasers directed straight at her.

"Don't," she said, shaking her head, sensing he was about to rail at her for disobeying his orders. "Don't," she repeated on a thin, tortured whisper as hot tears spilled down her cheeks and she started trembling so violently the rifle wavered in her hands.

Blue's solid, steady strength was at her side in a heartbeat. He snatched the gun and caught her against him just as her knees gave out.

"Duct tape," Blue said, after he'd used the tape to bind the last poacher's hands and feet. "Man's best friend. Next to you, of course, Hersh." He gave the lab an affectionate pat on his head. "Never knew you were such a tiger."

His gaze strayed then to Maggie, where she sat huddled against a tree trunk, her hair wild around her face, her eyes still glazed with threatening shock.

With a weary, concerned breath he went to her, hunkered down and touched a hand to her hair. "You okay?"

She nodded but wouldn't look at him. "Is he dead?" Her voice was as void of strength as her face was void of color.

"No, Stretch," he said gently. "He's not dead. But when he wakes up, his head's gonna hurt so bad, he'll wish he was. You pack a helluva wallop."

He'd hoped for a smile. Even a small one. What he got was a fresh round of silent tears.

"Come here," he said, feeling caught somewhere between anger and heartache.

This was the woman he loved. This was the woman who had just risked her life for him—yet was unable to risk loving him.

His heart beat out his frustration as he held her in the moonlight. Shielding her from the cool night air, he battled back a latent, gut-tightening fear that made him want to tear into her for her reckless actions that could have gotten her hurt or killed.

Yet all he did was hold her while he waited for Abel to return from the shore, where he'd set a bonfire as a beacon for the DNR to follow. He let his head rest against the tree and closed his eyes as silence swelled between them like a barrier.

It was with a sad and weary relief that he heard voices and knew the law had finally shown up.

They all had to give their statements. J.D. kept his eye on Maggie as he did most of the talking, Abel commenting only when asked a direct question.

J.D. watched her shiver when he told the DNR officers how he and Abel had found the tri-hauler and were in the process of disabling it when the poachers had caught them and forced them at gunpoint to their camp. His heart almost broke when she lowered her head between her updrawn knees as he related how they'd been close to getting shot when Hershey had leapt into the campsite like a hound from hell. The distraction had been enough for them to disarm one man and the rest was history.

By the time they finally left the island, she seemed to have gotten control of herself. At least the tears had stopped and the shaking had subsided to occasional tremors.

When they arrived back at her cabin, she insisted that both he and Abel sit at her kitchen table while she cleaned the cuts on their faces and knuckles with a silent but thorough attention to their needs.

Abel left shortly after, looking stunned and shaken when Maggie had thrown herself into his arms and held him for a long silent moment.

"Come on, Stretch," J.D. said softly as she stood at the window, looking lost and weary as she stared through the night toward the bay where Abel's boat cut through dark water, leaving a wide, rippling wake in its path.

"Come on," he repeated, taking her hand and leading her to the bedroom.

In silence he undressed her. She stood as docile as a kitten, lifting a foot when he asked, raising an arm when he gently prodded. He lowered her nightshirt over her head, turned back the covers and tucked her into bed.

"Stay with me," she whispered when he turned to leave the room.

His heart stilled. His grip tightened on the doorknob. He didn't have to see her eyes to know they shimmered with tears. He heard every one of them in her voice.

He hung his head, knowing he wasn't strong enough to go to her and not take her. Knowing that if he took her tonight, it would be with equal measures of love, desperation and anger.

In the aftermath of the violent events of this night, her inability to trust him and the pain her accusations caused came back with double-barreled force. It hammered at him until he wanted to shout at her to look at what she was throwing away.

But he couldn't shout at her tonight any more than he could leave her. Not like this.

"I'm not leaving you, Stretch. But I can't share your bed. Not without making love to you. And if I loved you now, I might hurt you."

His hands shook as he closed the door behind him. His heart thundered as he made a bed on the sofa and sank into it, feeling every bruise where a fist had pummeled his body.

He didn't sleep much that night. He lay in the dark, counted the stars and wondered where they would go from here.

In the morning, he had his answer.

She was gone. The only thing left of her was a two-word note she'd propped against a vase of wildflowers in the center of the kitchen table.

Leaving Blue had been the hardest thing Maggie had ever done. Harder even than returning to New York and confronting Rolfe. Harder than returning to the lake a week later and facing a cabin empty of everything but memories of the man who had taught her about love.

No one ever said life wasn't hard, she thought, battling cynicism as she walked in the sunlight to the dock. And no one ever said love wasn't worth fighting for. She just wished it hadn't taken her so long to figure it out.

The night before she'd left Blue, she'd lain in the dark, her only light that of the moon dancing on the water. Her only company was a troubled sleep in which every childhood nightmare she'd ever had came back as vivid and as frightening as their encounter with the poachers. It had been a long time since she'd feared snakes under the bed—a child's subconscious fear of the viperous unknowns of life.

She'd realized then that she had to give closure to her past and the unknown consequences of confronting Rolfe. Rolfe represented the snakes under her bed. Rolfe represented most of her demons, too, and ready or not, she had to exorcise them if she were to get on with her life. In those long, dark hours, she'd realized she couldn't put it off any longer.

And now it was done. A chill ran through her at the memory of the hatred in Rolfe's eyes. The anger in his words. The threats and contempt and the promises of retaliation.

And she remembered, with a source of pride she'd never known, how she'd stood up to him, promising retaliation of her own if he was foolish enough to make good on his threats. She'd been shaking inside the entire time. She hadn't let him see it. Just like she hadn't given in when his threats had turned to promises, the promises to sad, pathetic pleas.

She drew in a deep breath, lifted her head to the sun and felt the weight of her past lift and recede. Her present was what mattered now. Her present and her future with Blue.

She was determined there would be a future. Only it was beginning to look like she was the one who was going to have to initiate it.

She'd been back a week. The very first day, she'd heard the sound of the Cessna's engine fly over, then buzz the bay. Filled with hopes and joy, she'd scrambled out of the cabin, run out onto the dock and waved until she thought her arm was going to fall off.

He'd seen her. She had no doubt that he'd seen her. Yet she'd stood, one hand shading her eyes, the other at her throat, as the plane had grown smaller and smaller until it was only a fleck of silver against the cerulean sky, then disappeared completely. He hadn't been back since.

She'd hurt him. She knew she'd hurt him. The night she'd left, she'd composed a hundred different notes in her head to tell him what she had to do. In the end, no words seemed right. In retrospect, she realized he could have construed her hurriedly scribbled "trust me" to mean anything from "wait for me," to "I'll be back," to "goodbye." He'd had to live with that. And now, so did she.

The past seven days, she'd worked like a dog. She'd cleaned up, aired out, shined bright, listening for the plane, in her heart knowing he wouldn't return. And all the while she'd remembered and missed and longed for Blue's arms around her, Blue's smile caressing her, Blue's body loving her.

She drew solace from the water sounds and the bird song. She found small pleasures in the lazy drift of the faded red, white and blue wind sock fluttering in the breeze, in the soft droning buzz of hummingbirds flitting from the wild iris to the sweet williams in the flower bed bordering the forest.

Small pleasures, however, were no longer enough. After loving Blue, small pleasures would never be enough.

A loon sounded in the bay. She raised her head to the lonesome, mournful sound, tracking its solitary progress as it fished the shallow waters alone.

Alone. She didn't want to be alone anymore. And it struck her then that if she wanted to correct the situation, she was going to have to do something about it.

Her opportunity arrived the next morning when Abel drove his boat up to her dock.

"Will you take me to him?"

Like the friend he was, he didn't ask questions; he simply held out his hand and helped her into the boat.

J.D. had given her a new paint job. It was past time for a change. It was time for a lot of changes, J.D. thought grimly as he looked the Cessna up and down, satisfied with the shiny red enamel that now covered the fuselage and wingtips.

"What d'ya think, Al?" he asked the arthritic old man sitting on the dock, alternately inspecting the lures in his tackle box and swatting flies.

Al hitched his thumbs under the straps of his bib overalls, squinted over the top of his scratched half glasses and eyed the Cessna. "It'll do," he mumbled, giving the plane one last distracted look and going back to rummaging around in his tackle box.

"Your enthusiasm over...whelms...me..." J.D. said, his words trailing off when he recognized the boat pulling into the Crane Cove Marina—and the woman sitting in the bow.

His memory hadn't lived up to the reality—neither had his dreams. She was the most beautiful woman he'd ever seen. And even though it had only been a week since she'd left, seeing her again sent his heart rate off the charts.

He stood on a float, one hand gripping a wing strut, the other propped on his hip as she walked toward him, her dark hair wind-whipped and shining, her long legs tan and sleek beneath her white shorts, her eyes bright and expectant and not a little bit wary.

"Hey, Blue." Her voice was soft and tentative as she crossed her arms under her breasts in that giveaway action that relayed how nervous she was.

Hershey, who'd been sleeping like the dead in the shade of the boathouse, woke up with a start when he heard her voice. He jumped to all fours and ran at her like she'd brought his favorite bone.

"Hey, Stretch," J.D. said, and hoped she didn't hear the tremor in the words he'd tried too hard to make sound casual. "How's it going?"

Starting with the day he'd buzzed her bay and discovered she was back, he couldn't count the number of times he'd made up his mind to go to her—then let his pride muscle in and change his decision.

Only his pride kept him from going to her now, scooping her up in his arms and making love to her until he obliterated any argument she might still have that would keep them apart.

Instead, he worked his jaw and watched her.

She looked at him from where she'd dropped to her knees to hug Hershey. "Better now." Her dark eyes glistened when they met his. "Much better now."

Emotions he'd tucked away the day she'd left him seemed to swell and grow too large for the small closet that harbored his feelings. He'd intended to make this as hard for her as it was for him. He couldn't do it.

"How much better?" he asked, letting go of the strut and jumping from the float to the dock.

She managed a crooked smile. "Got a minute? I'll tell you all about it."

* * *

Sunlight slivered down through the whispering pine and trembling birch, dappling the forest floor with flickering light and dusky shadows. They walked slowly along the pine-needle-covered hiking trail that Blue had suggested they take so they could talk in private.

But even as determined as she was to share everything with him, it was still hard to know where to start.

"Why not at the beginning," he suggested gently, when she told him as much.

"The beginning," she echoed, and drew a deep breath. "I'm not sure I remember where the beginning is. Maybe it was when the courts took me out of my mother's home and placed me in the first of a string of foster homes." She shivered and wrapped her hands around her bare arms. "Maybe there never was a beginning—even though I kept waiting for one. Kids are funny that way. Resilient, you know?" She kept her head down, looking at her feet as she walked. "I kept thinking that since my mom didn't want me enough to clean up her act so she could keep me with her, that the next set of foster parents would be permanent ones and that would be the beginning of my terrific new life. Only it never worked out that way."

Blue remained silent, supportive beside her. She drew strength from that.

"That's one of the things I used to resent about you." She smiled tightly and angled a quick glance at him. "You had the perfect life. Parents who loved you. Money to do what you wanted. An ego that told anyone who knew you how secure you were with yourself and everyone around you."

"Peter Pan man, that's me," he said with a hint of disgust in his voice.

She stopped and faced him, taking his hands in hers, reveling in the feel of their callused yet gentle strength. "No. Don't ever feel you have to apologize for that. What you are, *who* you are, and how you got that way—all of that is what makes you special. I'm just trying to make you see where I was coming from. Where I *came* from. I don't want your pity or your sympathy—I just want you to know so you'll understand why I did what I did. And why I was so afraid to trust you."

She looked at their joined hands, looked at his face. His blue eyes were gentle, his face drawn with concern and a determined patience that gave her the courage to go on.

Keeping his hand in hers, she started walking along the path again.

"I was seventeen when I moved to New York. Tough as nails and figuring I could take anything that city could dish out. After all, I'd just survived the attentions of a foster father who had more than fatherly affection on his agenda." She drew a deep breath, and fought back the revulsion and shame that accompanied that particular ugly memory with a fonder one of the time she'd spent with the Snyders who had never been anything but kind to her, but because of system restraints, couldn't keep her permanently.

"Anyway," she continued, trying to ignore the sudden, almost violent clenching of Blue's hand around hers. "I was going to make it as a star on Broadway."

She smiled at her naiveté, remembering. "I ended up waiting tables and—" she hesitated, each word as hard as she'd anticipated, her smile fading with yet another dark memory "—I was close to resorting to other methods of making my rent money…"

She had to stop again and fight the helpless feeling that the desperate memory fostered before she could go on.

"Fortunately, I didn't have to go that route. And needless to say, I didn't make it as an actress, either. I was 'discovered' instead by a famous photographer."

"Sebastion . . . Rolfe Sebastion, wasn't it?" Blue's voice was tight. A frown creased his brows. "I followed your career, Maggie. Your story didn't miss many magazines."

She smiled ruefully. "Cinderella and her charming prince, right? Isn't that how the media liked to tell it? Only it turns out the prince wasn't so charming. At least he lost his charm as the years went by."

Beside her, she could feel Blue's tension mounting. She prayed he could forgive her for what she was about to tell him. Prayed that even though it would be painful, that she had the strength to see it through.

She drew a deep breath and bent to pick up a curling piece of birch bark, shredding it as they walked.

"The worst of it," she reflected aloud, "was that I let what he did to me happen. What I have to keep telling myself," she continued, digging deep for justification of how she had let Rolfe dominate her, "is that I was young. Young and needy. He was the first person who had ever taken an interest in me on a long-term basis. I saw him as my savior. I saw myself in love with him. Finally, someone cared about me. Finally, someone actually loved me. And in the name of love, I did anything he asked of me.

"Anything," she repeated as a rolling nausea tumbled through her. "Until it got to the point that he would go to great lengths to put me in positions where he could show the control he had over me."

She became very quiet then, her steps slowing until she stopped. Her throat clogged up. Tears she refused to shed welled in her eyes. "I . . . it was the day of my twenty-fifth birthday. I'd just found out I was pregnant. The news was going to be my birthday present to him."

She pinched her eyes shut and turned away. Blue's strong, warm hands on her shoulders gave her courage.

"It turned out he didn't much care for my present. In fact, he was livid. My career, he'd railed. A baby would

ruin my career. He wanted me to get an abortion.'' She
made a sound of pained despair.

"He *ordered* me to get an abortion. I refused. It was the
first time I'd ever defied him. Evidently, he felt the emotional abuse was no longer enough—because it was also the
first time he beat me.''

The warm hands on her shoulders tightened. She felt
Blue's tension as if it were her own and knew that his silence was as much from a tortured effort at control as it was
in support.

"He beat me so badly...the abortion was no longer an
issue.''

She'd known this was going to be painful. She hadn't
known the pain would consume her until the aching despair over the loss of her child crushed down like earth on
a shallow grave.

Her baby. He'd killed her baby. And she'd been too weak
to stop him. Self-directed anger ripped through her heart.

She didn't know when Blue had pulled her against him.
She was only aware of the crush of his arms around her, of
his solid strength enfolding her.

"When I recovered,'' she whispered against his shoulder, "I ran away from him. It didn't take long for him to
find me and bring me back. And I've hated myself every
day of my life for being so weak and letting him.

"Oh, I tried again. But again he followed, heaping on the
guilt, layering the promises, playing on my shame over letting him abuse me as additional leverage for his control.

"He'd made me what I was—famous, rich, a woman
who had everything—taking great pleasure in constantly
pointing out that if it wasn't for him, no one would care
about me. If it wasn't for my face and my body, no one
would have a reason to.''

"The bastard,'' Blue gritted out, wrapping her tighter
against him.

"Yes," she whispered, nestling against him, praying that more than sympathy fueled his actions. "He's a bastard. And among my many regrets is the fact that it took me so long to realize he'd been feeding his own insecurities by working on mine."

She pressed her forehead to his chest. "Two years ago, when I found out the Snyders had left me the cabin, I started formulating a plan. It took me eighteen months to secretly filter out fifty-thousand dollars in cash from my own accounts that Rolfe controlled and watched like a hawk. When the opportunity finally came, I packed light, paid cash for a four-wheel-drive Jeep and started driving.

"That was six months ago. I only decided to chance coming to the cabin after I'd made sure the last place he could trace me to was L.A. Then I dropped out of sight.

"And then you found me," she whispered, lifting her face to his. "And you made me feel special, and loved, and it scared me so much . . . it scared me so much, Blue," she murmured, touching her fingers to his cheek, "that I fought you, and denied you, and finally when you were getting so close to my heart I feared for it all over again, I blamed you for everything Rolfe and anyone else in my life who had ever used me had done."

His eyes glistened as they met hers. "I'll never, never hurt you, Maggie."

"I know," she whispered. "I know that now. And I'll never hurt you. Never again. That's why I had to leave you. I had to go back to New York and face him. More than anything, I wanted to be able to stop looking over my shoulder, wondering how long I had before he found me."

"Why didn't you tell me? Why didn't you let me help you?"

"Because this was my mess. My battle. And because if I didn't go back and fight it, I'd never be free of him."

His grip became fiercely protective. "That sonofabitch will never touch you again."

"You're right about that. He knows now that I've got my lawyers on alert. If he so much as breathes in my direction, I'll have him in court so fast he'll wish he never met me."

For the longest time he just held her, and rocked her, soothing his hand over her hair.

"I feel so ashamed," she choked out on a hoarse whisper. "I've been so weak."

"You've never been weak, Stretch. Never." He set her away from him, cupping her face in his hands. "What you've never been is loved. Not until you met me." His eyes searched hers, full of truth and love and promise. "I'll make up for all of them. I'll give you so much love, you'll forget it was ever lacking in your life.

"I'll give you babies," he promised. "All the babies you want."

The love and the pain and the giving in his words enveloped her with the most perfect sense of belonging she'd ever known. She searched his face and saw the heart of this Peter Pan man and knew he had the capacity to heal her.

"I love you, Blue Hazzard. So much. Will you marry me?"

He heaved a huge sigh and whispered against her mouth, "I thought you'd never ask."

Epilogue

It was a big wedding, a big, bright afternoon affair, an extravaganza worthy of the most romantic movie production Hollywood could ever stage. Blue insisted. He wanted all of his family and friends to meet his bride and see how happy he was and to share their special day.

If the congregation in the packed church thought it odd that the maid of honor wore a tuxedo and a blue silk ribbon to hold back his jet black hair, and that the ring bearer had four feet and a tail, they didn't say as much. They only smiled indulgently, some of them dabbing at their eyes as a glowing bride and an adoring groom exchanged vows and rings and a long, lingering kiss.

They flew in the Cessna from the Cities to Crimson Falls to honeymoon. Maggie insisted. Getting her into the plane was no longer a problem. Getting acres of shimmering ice blue satin and French lace into the cockpit was.

"I should have changed," she said with a laugh as Blue shoved the last of the billowing train inside and closed the cockpit door.

"Not on your life." His look left no room for debate when he climbed in the other side. Making sure Hershey was set in the back, he tugged his black tie loose, undid the top button of his pleated shirt and fired up the engine. "I'm only planning on one bride in my life, Stretch. And I'm only figuring on one wedding night. When that gown comes off, I'm going to be there."

A delicious shiver of anticipation sluiced through her blood in anticipation of the night ahead.

"Did I tell you yet how beautiful you look?" he added, his eyes going smoky and dark.

She leaned toward him, her eyes glistening with hope and love and a delicious, suppressed desire. "You're pretty beautiful yourself." She touched a hand to his hair, then threaded her fingers through the glorious golden mass of it and leaned in to his kiss.

A cold nose on her cheek had her pulling back with a laugh. "Yes, Hersh. You're pretty awesome, too. I don't know why your master couldn't have sprung for a new collar, though."

Blue angled his head around to study the collar in question. It was the same one Maggie had been holding when Hershey had bolted for the poacher. He'd repaired the torn leather with massive amounts of duct tape.

"He likes his collar that way, don't you, Hersh? It gives him kind of a macho, heavy-metal look—a must for all pit bull wannabes."

Maggie had to fight the urge to pinch herself as they flew north with the aid of a light tail wind and a cloudless sky. This much joy, this much rich, vital emotion was foreign to her. But she knew that her life with Blue would be full of everything it had been lacking before he came into it. She was going to enjoy getting used to the wonder of it all. Starting now.

"James Dean," she murmured.

"What? I didn't catch that." Blue angled a look her way, raising his voice to be heard above the engine's roar.

She leaned toward him with an amused grin. "I'd always wondered what J.D. stood for. I had to marry you to find out."

A crooked smile tilted his beautiful mouth. "So now you know where I get my romantic tendencies. My mother was completely enamored with James Dean during her pregnancy."

"Well, I'm completely enamored with him now." Her hand on his arm reinforced her words. He covered it with his own.

"I loved your family. Your mom and dad are wonderful. And your brother—he's even a bigger flirt than you are. I'll bet Sandy has to keep on her toes around him."

"Cary's all show. He's a big goon over Sandy and their girls. We Hazzard men cherish our women."

That night, sequestered in the honeymoon room at the Crimson Falls with nothing but a bed, a bottle of champagne and each other, he showed her just how much.

The gown, lovingly removed by strong yet gentle and exquisitely sensual hands, lay in a pale blue pool on the floor by the bed.

He made love to her like it was the first time, the only time, the last time, pleasing her, teasing her, prolonging her pleasure until she cried from the wondrous gift of his love.

"You'll pay for this, Hazzard," she murmured when she could find the strength. "You'll pay dearly."

He ran a hand along the silk of her back, close to exhaustion himself as he drew her snugly against his side. "I think you just stole my line. But go ahead, steal away. With you, Maggie mine, I've got a feeling paybacks will be heaven." Then he drifted off to sleep.

When J.D. woke up, his bride was sitting on the bed beside him, a roll of duct tape clutched in her hand. He blinked sleepily up at her, a smile rising at the flushed, rosy look of her in the darkened room.

"Beautiful," he murmured, wanting to brush back the fall of hair that tumbled across her face in a tangle of chestnut-colored satin. He tried to lift his hand, but couldn't move it.

He twisted his head around on the pillow, squinted and finally realized his wrist was taped to the brass head rail with duct tape. A moment later, it registered that his other wrist was bound, as well.

He met her eyes again, a question lurking in his. She answered with a beguiling look infused with mischief, passion and love.

"Payback time?" he ventured with a crooked, hopeful smile.

"Payback time," she whispered, sparking desire to fire through his blood and couple with the sweetest anticipation he'd ever known.

She set the roll of tape on the dresser by the bed, then, never taking her eyes from his, slowly draped her breathtaking, gloriously naked self on top of him.

He groaned at the delicious contact of her soft, supple heat pressing to his. Bit back a moan and strained against the constraints of the binding tape when she slid slowly against him, creating an explosive, erotic friction that stole his breath and made him moan.

"Duct tape," he breathed, barely able to mouth the words as he arched against her hands and her mouth as she did wonderful, wanton things to his body, "changed... my... life."

He felt her smile against his skin, felt himself sink completely under her spell as the moon peeked in through the open window, lining her with gold.

"I love you, Maggie."

"I know," she whispered, just before she drove him over the edge.

Later, much later, after his silver bonds had been broken and he'd pulled her beneath him, the groom wore a very satisfied smile—and the bride wore nothing but Blue.

* * * * *

The first book in the exciting new
Fortune's Children series is
HIRED HUSBAND
by *New York Times* bestselling writer
Rebecca Brandewyne

Beginning in July 1996
Only from Silhouette Books

Here's an exciting sneak preview....

Minneapolis, Minnesota

As Caroline Fortune wheeled her dark blue Volvo into the underground parking lot of the towering, glass-and-steel structure that housed the global headquarters of Fortune Cosmetics, she glanced anxiously at her gold Piaget wristwatch. An accident on the snowy freeway had caused rush-hour traffic to be a nightmare this morning. As a result, she was running late for her 9:00 a.m. meeting—and if there was one thing her grandmother, Kate Winfield Fortune, simply couldn't abide, it was slack, unprofessional behavior on the job. And lateness was the sign of a sloppy, disorganized schedule.

Involuntarily, Caroline shuddered at the thought of her grandmother's infamous wrath being unleashed upon her. The stern rebuke would be precise, apropos, scathing and delivered with coolly raised, condemnatory eyebrows and in icy tones of haughty grandeur that had in the past reduced many an executive—even the male ones—at Fortune Cosmetics not only to obsequious apologies, but even to tears. Caroline had seen it happen on more than one occasion, although, much to her gratitude and relief, she herself was seldom a target of her grandmother's anger. And she wouldn't be this morning, either, not if she could help it. That would be a disastrous way to start out the new year.

Grabbing her Louis Vuitton totebag and her black leather portfolio from the front passenger seat, Caroline stepped gracefully from the Volvo and slammed the door. The heels of her Maud Frizon pumps clicked briskly on the concrete floor as she hurried toward the bank of elevators that would take her up into the skyscraper owned by her family. As the elevator doors slid open, she rushed down the long, plushly carpeted corridors of one of the hushed upper floors toward the conference room.

By now Caroline had her portfolio open and was leafing through it as she hastened along, reviewing her notes she had prepared for her presentation. So she didn't see Dr. Nicolai Valkov until she literally ran right into him. Like her, he had his head bent over his own portfolio, not watching where he was going. As the two of them collided, both their portfolios and the papers inside went flying. At the unexpected impact, Caroline lost her balance, stumbled, and would have fallen had not Nick's strong, sure hands abruptly shot out, grabbing hold of her and pulling her to him to steady her. She gasped, startled and stricken, as she came up hard against his broad chest, lean hips and corded thighs, her face just inches from his own—as though they were lovers about to kiss.

Caroline had never been so close to Nick Valkov before, and, in that instant, she was acutely aware of him—not just as a fellow employee of Fortune Cosmetics but also as a man. Of how tall and ruggedly handsome he was, dressed in an elegant, pin-striped black suit cut in the European fashion, a crisp white shirt, a foulard tie and a pair of Cole Haan loafers. Of how dark his thick, glossy hair and his deep-set eyes framed by raven-wing brows were—so dark that they were almost black, despite the bright, fluorescent lights that blazed overhead. Of the whiteness of his straight teeth against his bronzed skin as a brazen, mocking grin slowly curved his wide, sensual mouth.

"Actually, I *was* hoping for a sweet roll this morning—but I daresay you would prove even tastier, Ms. Fortune," Nick drawled impertinently, his low, silky voice tinged with a faint accent born of the fact that Russian, not English, was his native language.

At his words, Caroline flushed painfully, embarrassed and annoyed. If there was one person she always attempted to avoid at Fortune Cosmetics, it was Nick Valkov. Following the breakup of the Soviet Union, he had emigrated to the United States, where her grandmother had hired him to direct the company's research and development department. Since that time, Nick had constantly demonstrated marked, traditional, Old World tendencies that had led Caroline to believe he not only had no use for equal rights but also would actually have been more than happy to turn back the clock several centuries where females were concerned. She thought his remark was typical of his attitude toward women: insolent, arrogant and domineering. Really, the man was simply insufferable!

Caroline couldn't imagine what had ever prompted her grandmother to hire him—and at a highly generous salary, too—except that Nick Valkov was considered one of the foremost chemists anywhere on the planet. Deep down inside, Caroline knew that no matter how he behaved, Fortune Cosmetics was extremely lucky to have him. Still, that didn't give him the right to manhandle and insult her!

"I assure you that you would find me more bitter than a cup of the strongest black coffee, Dr. Valkov," she insisted, attempting without success to free her trembling body from his steely grip, while he continued to hold her so near that she could feel his heart beating steadily in his chest—and knew he must be equally able to feel the erratic hammering of her own.

"Oh, I'm willing to wager there's more sugar and cream to you than you let on, Ms. Fortune." To her utter mortification and outrage, she felt one of Nick's hands slide insidiously up her back and nape to her luxuriant mass of sable hair, done up in a stylish French twist.

"You know so much about fashion," he murmured, eyeing her assessingly, pointedly ignoring her indignation and efforts to escape from him. "So why do you always wear your hair like this...so tightly wrapped and severe? I've never seen it down. Still, that's the way it needs to be worn, you know...soft, loose, tangled about your face. As it is, your hair fairly cries out for a man to take the pins from it, so he can see how long it is. Does it fall past your shoulders?" He quirked one eyebrow inquisitively, a mocking half smile still twisting his lips, letting her know he was enjoying her obvious discomfiture. "You aren't going to tell me, are you? What a pity. Because my guess is that it does—and I'd like to know if I'm right. And these glasses." He indicated the large, square, tortoiseshell frames perched on her slender, classic nose. "I think you use them to hide behind more than you do to see. I'll bet you don't actually even need them at all."

Caroline felt the blush that had yet to leave her cheeks deepen, its heat seeming to spread throughout her entire quivering body. Damn the man! Why must he be so infuriatingly perceptive?

Because everything that Nick suspected was true.

* * * * *

To read more, don't miss
HIRED HUSBAND
by Rebecca Brandewyne,
Book One in the new
FORTUNE'S CHILDREN series,
beginning this month and available only from
Silhouette Books!

New York Times Bestselling Author
REBECCA BRANDEWYNE

Launches a new twelve-book series—FORTUNE'S CHILDREN
beginning in July 1996 with Book One

Hired Husband

Caroline Fortune knew her marriage to Nick Valkov was in
name only. She would help save the family business, Nick
would get a green card, and a paper marriage would suit both
of them. Until Caroline could no longer deny the feelings Nick
stirred in her and the practical union turned passionate.

MEET THE FORTUNES—a family whose legacy is greater than
riches. Because where there's a will...there's a wedding!

Look for Book Two, *The Millionaire and the Cowgirl*,
by Lisa Jackson. Available in August 1996 wherever Silhouette
books are sold.

by Jackie Merritt

The Fanon family—born and raised in
Big Sky Country...and heading for a wedding!

Meet them in these books from
Silhouette Special Edition® and
Silhouette Desire® beginning with:

MONTANA FEVER
Desire #1014, July 1996

MONTANA PASSION
That Special Woman!
Special Edition #1051, September 1996

And look for more MADE IN MONTANA titles
in 1996 and 1997!

Don't miss these stories of ranching and love
only from Silhouette Books!

Silhouette®
™

MONTANA

Who can resist a Texan...or a Calloway?

This September, award-winning author
ANNETTE BROADRICK
returns to Texas, with a brand-new
story about the Calloways...

SONS OF TEXAS

Rogues and Ranchers

CLINT: The brave leader. Used to keeping secrets.

CADE: The Lone Star Stud. Used to having women
fall at his feet...

MATT: The family guardian. Used to handling
trouble...

They must discover the identity of the mystery
woman with Calloway eyes—and uncover a
conspiracy that threatens their family....

Look for **SONS OF TEXAS:** Rogues and Ranchers
in September 1996!

Only from Silhouette...where passion lives.

You're About to Become a

Privileged Woman

Reap the rewards of fabulous free gifts and benefits with proofs-of-purchase from Silhouette and Harlequin books

Pages & Privileges™

It's our way of thanking you for buying our books at your favorite retail stores.

✂

```
┌─────────────────────────────┐
│ 📖  PROOF OF           │ SD-PP156
│     PURCHASE           │
│ Offer expires October 31, 1996 │
└─────────────────────────────┘
```

Harlequin and Silhouette—
the most privileged readers in the world!

For more information about Harlequin and Silhouette's PAGES & PRIVILEGES program call the Pages & Privileges Benefits Desk: 1-503-794-2499

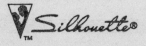

Silhouette®

SD-PP156